WAR COMES HOME TO WINTHROP MANOR

War Comes Home to Winthrop Manor

An English Family Saga

Book Two:
Winthrop Manor Series

Mary Christian Payne

ISBN: 978-1-63161-058-5

Sign up for the newsletter to get news, updates and new release info from Mary Christian Payne:
www.TCKPublishing.com/mary

Published by TCK Publishing
www.TCKPublishing.com

Get discounts and special deals on books at
www.TCKPublishing.com/bookdeals

To Larry, for his creativity

CONTENTS

1

⚘

O n a spectacular English day, with clouds drifting aimlessly through the sky and the wind a gentle breeze, Lady Josephine, wife of Viscount Winterdale, known as "Win" to friends and family, felt strangely anxious. She gazed out a mullioned window while standing in the immense, lavishly decorated drawing room in Win's parental home, Winthrop Manor. Blue skies, daffodils, and a misty veil of newly formed leaves carried her back in time. Josephine cherished the memory of the endearing words Win had spoken before a never-to-be forgotten kiss on that other unforgettable spring day in 1914. They had pledged deep, everlasting love, and in spite of a wretched war, along with myriad other heartaches, their passion had endured. *Was it possible that eleven years had passed so quickly?*

Mrs. Shellady, Winthrop Manor's housekeeper, interrupted Josephine's reverie as she bustled into the room. "Good afternoon, Lady Josephine. I've not seen you since early this morning. You look to be wool-gathering, milady."

"Oh, Mrs. Shellady, I've been thinking about a day so reminiscent of this one. It was nineteen fourteen, and Win had kissed me for the first time. It's wonderful to have such cherished memories. I'd never even seen Winthrop Manor then, and now I've grown to love it so, not because of its splendour, though no one can deny its remarkable beauty, but because I so adore history, and Winthrop Manor has played such an important role throughout England's past. I'm so glad Win and I made the decision to move back here after his return from the war."

"Yes, I am too," answered Mrs. Shellady. "All of the staff feel the same way."

"Eventually, we would have had to return anyway," Josephine continued, "given the rapid decline in the earl's health." Win's father had grown frail and weak.

"Yes, I know," Mrs. Shellady replied. "I think, deep in my heart, I've always believed there would be a reconciliation between Win and his parents. They always adored him, and it was unthinkable that they would continue the ridiculous estrangement forever."

"Yes. I was convinced of that too," Josephine replied. "You're probably aware that the falling out between Win and his parents resulted from his marrying me." She smiled. "I'm sure they were disappointed their son married a commoner. As horrible as it is to say, Oliver's vicious kidnapping of our son did bring about the reconciliation." Josephine laughed aloud. "Oliver, the quintessential example of an aristocrat."

"It *is still* nearly impossible to imagine, isn't it?" Mrs. Shellady responded. "My goodness, milady. What if Oliver's belief that our Win had been killed in the war had been true? It still sends shivers down my spine to think of his diabolical scheme. Your precious son would have been adopted by that couple in London, having no idea that the little one had been stolen from his own brother. Oliver would have gone on to become the next Earl of Winthrop when his father passed. It's too wretched to even imagine. Of course, that could only have happened if Win *hadn't* returned from the Great War. Thank the good Lord he did."

Josephine turned and walked to sit on the sofa in front of the massive fireplace. "I truly don't think I could have survived such horror." Tears welled in her eyes. "I don't mean to sound hateful toward Win's parents. Truly, I don't. I've grown quite fond of them. Still, the entire alienation was so foolish."

"It all sorted itself out, milady." The housekeeper patted Josephine on the shoulder. "I hope Oliver spends the rest of his life behind bars. I never want to lay my eyes upon him again."

"Nor do I," echoed Josephine.

It hadn't taken long after Win's return from fighting in France, and his resultant confinement in a German *Offizierlager* camp, for him to realise that his father's health was rapidly-declining. Lord Winthrop was no longer capable of meeting the demands required of an earl. Thousands of acres of land, a prodigious amount of livestock, and an enormous manor had to be overseen. Even though Winthrop Manor had ample staff, it was abundantly clear that an extensive amount of supervision was required to keep the estate lucrative. Those duties had now fallen upon Win.

Even four years after the war, many necessary tasks had been left unattended. The house was badly in need of a new roof. Due to its unusual serrated design, as well as its enormity, the cost would be astronomical. Both the exterior and interior needed painting–two other massive undertakings. At one time, such necessities weren't looked upon as worrisome, but reduced financial circumstances had taken a toll on nearly all upper-class families following the war.

A combination of the cost of war, death duties, disabling taxes, and a downturn in farm rentals had brought an end to a life of refined beauty and feudal rights, as well as duties and privileges previously enjoyed by Britain's landed gentry. British Prime Minister David Lloyd-George's government was struggling to cope with the cost of paying for the unrestrained expenses of war, while also meeting demands of the returning heroes for homes and jobs. The Earl of Winthrop, as a member of the House of Lords, was searching for ways to contend with the nation's woes, as well as his own.

"I hate to sound anxious and worried on such a splendid day, Mrs. Shellady, but I can't help but be concerned about our monetary situation," Josephine said. "Many of the Great Houses are being forced to open their doors to the public for a fee. That seems such an awful thing to do."

"Oh, milady! Is the situation that bad at Winthrop Manor?" Mrs. Shellady asked. It was a rather personal conversation to have with a housekeeper, yet Josephine was very close with her. From the beginning of their relationship, when Josephine and Win moved back to the manor, she and Mrs. Shellady had become more like two dear friends than employer and employee. There *were* facts, of course, that would never be shared with a member of the staff. Josephine, however, was only too aware of them, and they weighed heavily upon her. A long chat with Win was necessary.

Just as she contemplated the topics they needed to discuss, Win entered the room. "So here you are, my beautiful wife," he murmured as he bent and kissed the back of her swan-like neck.

Mrs. Shellady greeted him before quietly exiting the drawing room.

Josephine still sat on the sofa. "Win, I'm worried," she said. "We need to have a serious chat."

"What about, my pet?"

"Have you looked at the account books lately?"

"Oh, indeed I have, Josephine. They're a dismal sight. Our property tax took more than a quarter of the estate's income from rents in this year, as compared to only four percent in nineteen-nineteen. As a whole, the burden of taxation on Winthrop Manor, including land tax rates and income tax, rose from nine to thirty percent of our income. I'm not sure we won't have to sell off some of the land," he continued. "Neither my father nor I have ever allowed such ghastly thoughts to enter our minds. The entire family, as well as our long-time retainers who've worked at Winthrop Manor since before I was born, will all have to pull together to maintain this large, stately home. The numbers of our male staff are severely diminished, due to so many having lost their lives in the war. There's also been a downturn in the number of those willing to serve in great houses like Winthrop Manor as their families have for hundreds of years. The war has forced so many women out of domestic service and into factories or offices. I've mentioned this dilemma to Radcliffe. He concurs." Radcliffe was the long-time butler at Winthrop Manor, who was always included in any discussion regarding matters, both large and small, which could affect employees. "He strongly feels we're going to have to raise wages for all of our employees or lose them to more lucrative careers," Win said.

"Well, darling, then that's what we'll do," Josephine answered, in a rather cheerful voice. Win had been educated at Eton and Oxford, and was a highly intelligent man. Nevertheless, Josephine understood his inability to fathom that his world was rapidly changing and would undoubtedly continue to do so. She knew his concerns could be easily done away with if she revealed facts Win should have known long before.

Win continued speaking, trying to explain the conundrum facing them. Her cheerful response seemed to concern him.

"Josephine, I don't believe you fully grasp the situation. In the past, the servants in great houses like ours were people whose family tradition was to work here. When someone left, the cook recommended her niece or younger sister. However, that no longer happens. So, there's a crisis in terms of the labour required to continue our lifestyle."

"Win, are you telling me that you believe our magnificent home is facing the threat of being sold or perhaps opened to the public for a fee? Are you certain you've gone over the figures carefully and there's absolutely no doubt about what will have to be done?"

"I'm going to sit down with financial advisers to sort out exactly what the situation is and what must be done. I've never excelled in fiscal matters or business enterprise. You know that. Sometimes I feel quite useless," he replied.

"Win, that's foolish. Neither one of us has ever been faced with concerns of a financial nature." Josephine was uncertain about what to say next. "Your favorite pastime is riding Black Orchid and attending equestrian races. Mine is tending roses. Neither qualifies us as experts in finance." She smiled, stood, and walked back to the window. He joined her there, where once again she gazed at the marvellous spring day. Sighing in frustration, she turned and embraced him. It was obvious that the only solution was for her to reveal facts she'd kept hidden from him.

She wasn't fearful of revealing the truth to her husband. Win was the kindest, most understanding man she'd ever known. She had no reason to worry that he might become angry or view the fact that she'd not shared vitally important information as dishonest. The truth was that Josephine harboured feelings of guilt, because she'd never mentioned the significant inheritance she'd received when her parents perished aboard the *Titanic*. She'd never shared this information with Win primarily because her Uncle Roderick, who had been her and Andrew's guardian, had advised her to save her money for a rainy day. It was abundantly clear that the rainy day had arrived.

Uncle Roderick trusted Win implicitly, and his intention had never been to construct a barrier between Josephine and her husband by advising her not to reveal her true financial situation. Roderick had simply held firm to the belief that a woman should have her own private cache of money in case an emergency presented itself. Josephine could clearly see that an emergency was facing them now.

"Win, I need to explain a matter of financial importance to us. I should have done so long ago, but Uncle Roderick felt it wiser for me to keep this information to myself. I *do* hope you aren't angry when I tell you now."

"Josephine, if Roderick gave advice on this matter, and you followed it, I cannot imagine being upset. You're well aware that I think the world of him. He looked after you and Andrew with great care, and I'm sure he always made wise decisions."

"Yes. I feel that way too," she answered. "Come Win, let's sit down where we'll be comfortable. Shall I ask Radcliffe to bring us tea?"

"I think I'd rather wait until I hear what you have to tell me. I may want something stronger," Win answered with a hint of amusement.

"I've never spoken to you about my inheritance. When Andrew and I lost our parents, we received a rather vast sum of money."

"What do you consider a *vast sum*?" For all he knew, the amount might be rather paltry. He had no idea whether she comprehended what constituted an inheritance of prodigious proportions.

"The executor of the estate was my father's business adviser and also a banker. He invested the money very conservatively at my father's request. Over the years, it has grown considerably. The last time we spoke, he informed me that the entire portfolio is worth over eight hundred thousand pounds. When Andrew died in the war, his portion became mine as well."

"My God, Josephine. That's a bloody fortune!" he exclaimed.

"Win, please don't curse. You know I don't like it," she said softly.

"I'm sorry, darling. I was momentarily shocked. Where is the money now? Is it invested in your name?"

"Yes. So, you see, we really *are* quite wealthy. Of course, this doesn't mean we can go on a wild spending spree. I tend to be rather cautious about finances, as you know. My father worked long and hard to leave such a fortune. With proper management, Winthrop Manor should be safe for Andy to take the reins someday and hopefully for his children down through the generations. I *do* hope you aren't distressed that I've waited until now to share this news with you, Win."

"No, Josephine, not at all. Roderick was sensible with his advice. I *do* feel that the acquisition should be managed carefully. Father has an excellent financial adviser in London. We should make an appointment to see him."

"Oh, Win, I would rather not do that," Josephine stated quite firmly. "Uncle Roderick has done a superb job of watching over my inheritance, and if I were to move it to another firm now, I'm afraid it would hurt him terribly. Also, while I don't like to think about it, my uncle isn't a young man any longer. He has also amassed a considerable fortune. He owns thousands of acres of land in and around Winthrop-on-Hart. Since he and Aunt Thelma were never fortunate enough to have children., he's made it quite clear to me that I'm the sole beneficiary of his estate. If we were to ask another professional to oversee my inheritance, Uncle just might decide we've inherited quite enough already. He could very easily change his mind and leave his estate to charity. I think it would be much wiser to leave things as they are."

"Yes, yes, of course you're correct," Win responded. "I've never expected any inheritance from Roderick. He's always lived so modestly."

"Yes, he has never been a money-motivated individual. He told me long ago that he wanted to be certain of security in his old age, and after that, his primary concern was that Andrew and I were never in want. Of course, that was before we lost Andrew. If he and Elisabeth had borne a child, I imagine Roderick would have set aside a significant portion of his estate for the baby, but that was never to be.

"At any rate, Tom is quite able to provide for her, as well as any child they may have in the future. I should also add that Uncle Roderick has left half of his estate to Andy. He and your father have had many long conversations, and apparently your father is most concerned that Andy need never worry about obtaining a fine education nor have any doubt that Winthrop Manor will continue to be one of England's most impressive great houses."

Win sat back and breathed a sigh of relief. He *had* been concerned. He'd concealed important financial matters from Josephine too, but with the news of her windfall, everything would now be on guaranteed footing. He would be able to tell her everything. They could begin again.

"I'm happiest about this because it means Andy will have the future we've both always wanted for him. I presume eventually we'll add to our family, and this incredible windfall will mean we can do so without concern about the costs associated with schooling, nannies, travel abroad, and the like. I *do* feel there's no need to share this news with *my* family, unless you disagree," he added.

"I'll follow your wishes regarding that," Josephine answered.

"If Elisabeth asks how I'm able to afford the necessary repairs here at the Manor, which is unlikely, I may be forced to mention that your father left a generous legacy. If that *does* happen, I have no intention of going into all of the details, nor the amount."

"Yes. I'm in agreement with you. I certainly *do not* want Oliver to ever know anything about our financial affairs."

"You needn't worry there, my pet," Win smiled. "As far as I'm concerned, Oliver will never set foot on Winthrop Manor property again. However, I *do* believe my parents should know we're secure."

"Yes, indeed. I agree."

Win truly meant to go further into facts about his own financial dilemma, but he decided he would wait a few more days. Perhaps, if he were fortunate, Josephine would never have to know.

Not many weeks after that conversation, Win and Josephine were jarred awake by sobs, screams, and hysterical weeping. Win slipped out of bed, running toward his parents' bedchamber, located in the west wing of the house. Josephine slipped on her robe and slippers and followed her husband.

Upon arrival in the earl and countess's room, they found a horrible scene. Win's father was lying on the bed, gurgling and making strange sounds. It was as though he was trying to communicate but couldn't form the words. The left side of his face drooped downward and only one eye was open. He thrashed 'round on the bed and nothing anyone said or did could calm him.

Lady Beatrice was beside herself, screaming at Win to do something.

He ran to the bedside table, grabbed the telephone, and asked the operator to connect him with Tom Drew. His chum from Oxford days was now his brother-in-law having married Win's sister Elisabeth, after her first husband, Andrew Chambers, Josephine's brother, was killed in the Great War. Tom and Elisabeth lived in Cloverdale, the next village over from Winthrop-on-Hart.

When Tom's sleepy voice came on the line, Win gave him a quick rundown of the facts. Tom said that he would be at Winthrop Manor in a matter of minutes.

By then, the old earl had ceased to thrash about and was lying quite still. He was breathing, but his breaths came in ragged gasps. He was making a supreme effort to speak, but it was impossible to understand what he was saying. The only intelligible words were, "Never lose the manor." It was clear that Win's father believed he was dying.

Win sat on the edge of the bed, holding his father's hand, and Lady Beatrice sat on the opposite side, tears streaming down her face as she choked back sobs.

"Oh Rupert, my darling. I've always loved you so. Please, please don't leave me. I need you, dearest," she whimpered.

Such a show of feeling rather surprised Josephine, since Win's mother had never been the sort to show emotion. Josephine never would have considered her in-law's marriage a love match. Nevertheless, in this tragic moment, Lady Beatrice's words gave proof that there had been real affection between them.

Tom Drew appeared in the doorway only moments later. He made straight for the patient. Utilising his stethoscope, he carefully listened to the earl's heart. He then placed the instrument on each side of the patient's neck. Finally, he turned and spoke to Lady Beatrice.

"I'm terribly sorry to have to tell you this, Lady Beatrice, but your husband has suffered a severe stroke. Did he complain earlier of a headache or numbness anywhere?"

"Yes," replied Lady Winthrop. "When the trouble first began, he threw his hands to his forehead and cried out, 'My God, my head!'"

"I'm not surprised," Tom replied. "There could be several reasons for this. I'm sorry to tell you, but he is not a candidate for surgery, as I suspect he will expire quite soon. He has a very slow, faint heartbeat. I'm going to give him an injection of morphine to alleviate any pain he's experiencing. Are we in agreement?" he asked.

There was a moment of silence. Finally, Win spoke. "Yes, Tom. Please make him as comfortable as possible. He wouldn't want to live as a vegetable, and I suspect that's what the outcome would be if he were to survive this."

"Right you are. The chances of survival are very, very slim." Tom filled a syringe and injected fluid into the earl's upper arm.

Almost at once the earl's body relaxed, and he looked more as though he was sleeping comfortably than facing death.

Lady Beatrice had stopped sobbing and sat staring at her husband's face, a stoic look on her own, holding his hand.

Tom continued to monitor the heart with his stethoscope. It was only moments later when the earl turned his head to the left on the pillow, taking one last breath.

"He's gone, milady," Tom said.

"God rest his soul." She leaned over and kissed her husband.

"Goodbye, Father. I'll follow your wishes. Winthrop Manor will continue to be the splendid estate it's always been," Win whispered.

Elisabeth stood by her father's side, looking bereft. "Dear Daddy. You were so special to me. As long as I'm alive on this earth, you will continue to be, since you'll always be in my heart." She began to weep.

Josephine reached over and took hold of her husband's hand. The earl had been kind to her. She took the old man's hand in hers. "I loved you, milord," she whispered into his ear. "I intend to raise my son to follow your footsteps. Rest in peace." Tears streamed down her cheeks.

"I'll contact the mortician," Tom said.

2

❧❧

Win's father was interred in the family mausoleum, outside of the chapel attached to Winthrop Manor. A space remained for his wife of over fifty years to be laid to rest next to him. Lady Beatrice had always been the picture of health, and there was no reason for anybody to assume she would follow her husband into the hereafter for a long time to come.

It came as a shock to the family, therefore, that not even a month later Lady Beatrice came down with the deadly flu virus that had ravaged the globe during the last year, killing more people than had died in the entire four years of fighting. The terrible pandemic had appeared to have waned when Lady Beatrice was struck with the well-recognised symptoms. In the morning, she'd accompanied her maid to the garden to clip some roses to brighten the dining table in the dower house, where she'd moved after losing her husband. By evening, her temperature had soared, and she was showing signs of terrible chest congestion, coughing unrelentingly. By midnight, her heart stopped beating. Win was stunned at the rapidity with which he had lost both parents. Another funeral was hastily arranged, and the late Countess and Earl of Winthrop lay side-by-side in the mausoleum outside of the ancient chapel.

Life as the new countess and earl at Winthrop Manor was tedious for Josephine and Win. Neither had expected to take on such responsibilities at their young ages, even though they had shouldered much of the responsibility since Win's return from the war. Josephine was then just twenty-four years old and Win was thirty. England had seen many changes following 1914. The class structure had begun to shift, as gentry and working man struggled side-by-side in the despicable trench warfare during the Great War. As a result, barriers between the classes tumbled. Many members of the serving class, who'd earned their keep by long-held positions in the homes of aristocrats, left those jobs and accepted better, higher-paying positions in factories. Additional facilities had sprung up to meet demands of a country at war. Women had taken jobs men had previously held when sons, husbands, and fathers were called upon to defend their country. Win and Josephine were more fortunate than many, for their loyal staff remained at Winthrop Manor. Josephine's inheritance had been able to provide the large sum needed to keep Winthrop Manor afloat, which meant that the young couple hadn't found themselves in the quandary many of the owners of great houses throughout England were facing.

Win *did* inherit money when his parents passed away, but he was somewhat shocked to learn that there was not nearly as much as had been anticipated. Even with Oliver having been cut off without a penny as a result of his dreadful plan to kidnap young Andy, Win was surprised to learn that he would not be receiving a large sum. Thank God for Josephine's inheritance.

Win's parents had not been frugal with finances, having paid little attention to what they'd spent. Lady Beatrice had been particularly extravagant, believing it a necessity to redecorate the house every three years. It also had been tremendously important for her to travel to Paris for the spring couture fashion shows each year. In addition, Win's father had put thousands of pounds into expensive horseflesh and fancy automobiles.

Thus, once again, Josephine was forced to put her skills with numbers to use. Due to her acumen, along with her own inheritance, Winthrop Manor was able to pull through. To keep their loyal and long-serving staff, Josephine made certain each person was given a significant increase in wages. At long last, all was in order, and while the family did not live the luxurious lifestyle as before the war, the large estate was on solid footing by 1925.

Win was enjoying the freedom to follow other pursuits. Before the war, he'd held little interest in nightlife, but the deplorable time spent as a POW, not to mention his memories of gruesome trench warfare, had altered him. Since the war's end, many men his age had returned with vastly different attitudes. Josephine hadn't noticed any profound change in her husband immediately after his return in 1916, following his escape from the POW camp.

He'd been wounded in the foot with the bayonet, but as time passed, the injury healed. He walked with a slight limp, which only added to his charm, since it signified that he had endured hardship during the Great War. He was so pleased to be on English soil again, able to be with his precious wife and their newborn son, that he'd had no desire to leave the peace and solitude of Winthrop Manor. Following his parents' deaths, he found himself fully occupied with the need to learn everything necessary to oversee such a massive estate.

As more and more leisure time became available to him, he began making frequent trips to the family townhouse on Curzon Street in Mayfair for weekend getaways with chaps who were of like mind. Private clubs were springing up throughout the city, and Win began to make frequent use of them, much to Josephine's dismay. His particular favourite for gambling, dancing, drinking, and jazz was The Pussy Cat Club, which had full-time bands playing day and night, seven days a week. It also had a reputation for many kinds of debauchery.

Win began to spend more and more time at the family townhouse, located in the heart of Mayfair, a highly prestigious area for wealthy landowners. Win's parents had purchased their second home on posh Curzon Street in the late 1800s. It had become the perfect spot to settle during the months of the Season, from May to July, or simply when the couple felt a need for a getaway to the capital city.

Now, in the same vicinity, the most fashionable, privileged club in London had popped up. Located in the heart of the West End, in the cellar of a deluxe building, The Pussy Cat Club had its primary entrance on Haymarket. The structure enveloped an entire complex, consisting of a large, embellished theater, as well as the social club itself. It was an ultra-stylish, members-only club, described as "deluxe, but wonderfully homelike"–an immensely patronised and posh night spot. Such was its popularity that within a short space of time, membership exceeded six thousand–including princes, cabinet ministers, dukes, and their peers. All London clubs were packed every night with the aristocracy, both affluent and notable.

Josephine paid scant attention to their emergence. She'd never found enjoyment in such settings and had never cared for the society life enjoyed by so many Londoners. Nor did she follow the latest gossip regarding "Bright Young Things," as the newspapers dubbed the "it" girls among young debutantes of the era. For that matter, Win had never shown much interest in such pursuits either, except when an occasional opening of a well-thought-of West End play occurred.

Nevertheless, as years passed between the end of the war and the rejuvenation of London as a city of fashionable, voguish style, Josephine was astounded to realise the changes that her husband's personality had undergone. Win—who had always been so levelheaded, trustworthy, and mature—had begun to act in an increasingly immature manner. It was no wonder she'd never conceived the baby she so desired, since her husband was seldom at Winthrop Manor in the evenings.

He would spend his days at the office on their property, working with the land agent and accountant, riding across their acreage on Black Orchid and enjoying a cocktail before dinner with his wife. Their chauffeur would then drive him to London for an evening of revelry.

While such activities held appeal for Win, he didn't completely forget that Josephine was waiting for him at the manor. He felt some guilt for the nights he spent away from his wife. It wasn't that he didn't love her, for he most certainly did. In fact, he truly wished that she would agree to join him in delightful evenings at the clubs.

On the other hand, when he was having a bad evening and thousands of pounds were lost to other men at the poker table, he was thankful Josephine *wasn't* present to see such demeaning and heartbreaking defeat. No matter his wishes, his wife had absolutely no interest in London nightlife and had grown to love Winthrop Manor with all her heart.

Like a great number of chaps who'd fought in the Great War, Win had witnessed depravity he'd never dreamed of. He spoke little of the horrors he'd seen. Men with intestines spilling out of their abdomens when they were annihilated beneath a hail of gunfire; decapitations from grenades thrown by Huns, soldiers left with nothing but shattered body parts. Sights too horrible to ever speak of. Win had buried his best friend and brother-in-law, Andrew, following convulsions brought about from dreadful, chemical gas used by the Huns in their attempt to defeat the English and Allied Forces.

Such atrocities had caused Win to see the world in a different light. Win knew that Josephine made every effort to take the horrors of the War into account. He strongly suspected that she never criticized his frequent absences from Winthrop Manor, for fear of causing him to justify himself by relating the shock he had gone through.

Unbeknownst to Josephine, an even larger problem loomed on the horizon. Win had developed a true obsession with gambling. Poker was a popular pastime for the chaps who gathered at the nightspots. Win had never held any great affinity for the game. However, during his time in the German POW camp, prisoners had turned to the card game as a means of passing time. They used matchsticks as currency.

When money became the medium of exchange, Win discovered a heightened enjoyment and developed an addiction to it. On one particular evening at The Pussy Cat Club, he gathered his winnings and was stunned to discover that they amounted to over twenty thousand pounds. The thrill he felt as he cashed in his chips was like nothing he had experienced before. It was as though he'd taken a powerful drug—one of which he could never get enough.

From that time on, poker became an obsession for the young earl. He lost more than he won, but when he *did* rake in a large pile of chips, he felt an indescribable thrill. He said nothing to his wife about the new pastime. He knew she would have been distressed to learn he was squandering money in such a fashion, particularly after she had given up her inheritance to keep them from losing Winthrop Manor.

Win fantasised about arriving home one day with an enormous fortune. He could picture presenting the money to Josephine, thereby paying back everything she had sacrificed to restore the manor, plus payment of exorbitant taxes and a re-establishment of their lifestyle. He could almost see the expression on her lovely face when he showed her his windfall. Unfortunately, that day never arrived.

A different sort of day *did* arrive, however, and with it came extreme heartbreak and anxiety for Josephine. She questioned whether she would be able to withstand the pain. She learned the vile details by complete accident while chatting with a lady friend she'd known for years. They'd met on the High Street in Winthrop-on-Hart, while Josephine was shopping for a baby gift meant for a dear friend from her school days. She encountered her old chum, Barbara Stanley, when they happened to be standing at the same counter in one of the village's upscale shops, dedicated to selling infant and children's goods.

"Well, for heaven's sake," exclaimed Barbara. "I haven't seen you in donkey's years, Josephine. Am I still allowed to address you by your given name? I heard you'd become a countess."

"Don't be absurd, Barbara. When did you ever know me to be enamoured by titles?"

"I'm only jesting," Barbara laughed. "I knew you wouldn't turn into a toff."

Josephine had known Barbara from their early school days together. Barbara had been raised on a much lower socioeconomic level than Josephine but had married a rather well-to-do farmer and now lived a comfortable life. Of course, it was certainly nothing the likes of Josephine and Lord Winthrop's, and Josephine sensed a bit of envy while speaking to her old friend.

"How have you been, Barbara?" Josephine asked. "You're looking splendid."

"Thank you, Josephine. So are you. Of course, I'd expect it of you. It's hard to imagine you going from living in your uncle's little cottage to becoming the countess at Winthrop Manor. My, how our lives do change." She smiled.

"Yes. I would never have predicted such a thing either. Of course, if I hadn't fallen head-over-heels for my husband, I would very likely never have ended up a countess."

"That reminds me," continued Barbara, "I saw your husband last week in London."

"Really? Where would that have been?" Josephine asked curiously.

"He was leaving that fancy club everyone is talking about—The Pussy Cat. Naturally, Ethan, my husband, and I aren't members. We just happened to be in the neighbourhood. It's then we spotted your husband—isn't his name Win?"

"Yes, that's right. His close friends call him that," Josephine replied.

"Yes, well, he was leaving the club. He was with a rather young woman. She was dressed in the new fashion—one of those short dresses, with fringe—you know the sort. I suppose she'd be known as a flapper. He was hailing a taxicab and having quite a time, as several people were leaving at the same time. He seemed to give up after a spell, and a beautiful Rolls-Royce, complete with chauffeur, drove to where he and the young lady were standing. I assume it was his personal vehicle."

"Yes, it would have been. When Win travels to London, our driver, David, takes him."

"Yes, well…actually, perhaps I shouldn't tell you this, but he kissed her once they settled into the auto."

Josephine could feel the colour drain from her face.

3

❧❧

Later that day, Josephine stood at the mullioned window overlooking the neatly cut lawn behind the ancient home. It was April 1925. She gazed at the beauty of the landscaping, while observing her ten-year-old son, Andy, playing with his beloved terrier, Twist. He would throw a ball and Twist would retrieve it, trotting back to Andy.

Josephine absolutely adored her son. It seemed he had grown up in such a short time, and she was keenly aware that soon he would be starting his first year of school at the Winfield Academy, the exclusive day-school, in Winthrop-on-Hart. Until that moment, it had never dawned upon her how quickly time passed.

She turned and paced the length of the drawing room. It was nearing time for dinner. Soon she would retreat to her bedchamber to change into a formal gown, the usual style of dress at Winthrop Manor for the evening meal.

Win would be returning from a day spent with financial advisers and would also retreat to his chamber to bathe and dress for the evening. Generally, he *did* dine with Josephine at the manor, but for quite some time he'd begun to depart shortly after the servants removed the dessert plates, saying that he had appointments in London.

Josephine wasn't a fool. She may not have grown up in an aristocratic setting, but she was well aware that her husband had *no* appointments of any necessity in the evenings—especially those lasting far into the wee hours.

She was certain that he was about to head to The Pussy Cat Club, and such knowledge filled her with concern. Perhaps most importantly, Josephine was frightened that her life with Win might never return to its original quiet existence. She had always trusted him implicitly. Josephine was certain, beyond any shadow of a doubt, that he would never cheat on her. Still, she didn't care for the existing situation. A married man belonged with his family, not gallivanting 'round London until the wee hours. Having met and spoken with Barbara Stanley earlier in the day, she was even more concerned.

Uncle Roderick had been Josephine's guardian since the loss of her parents, and she thought of him as a father. She asked the Winthrop Manor chauffeur, to drive her from the village to Roderick's cottage. She poured her heart out to her uncle. Roderick held her in his arms as she wept, admitting all the fears buried inside.

"Oh, my dear, dear Josephine. Win is a good man. I've always admired him. I never hesitated to grant my approval when you made the decision to marry. I can't say I'm terribly surprised at the behaviour you're now describing. The poor young men who fought in the war saw and experienced wretched things. At a time when they should have been enjoying their youth, they were thrust into a most abysmal situation. My only true amazement is that this behaviour has taken a rather prolonged time to manifest itself. I would have assumed these traits might have come out directly after he was mustered from the Expeditionary Forces."

"Yes, I agree." Josephine nodded. "Nevertheless, Win was every bit as loving and dear as he'd always been when he returned. Of course, the explanation for that may be that he was faced with so many challenges immediately upon his return. Andy's kidnapping, his brother Oliver's trial, and then the death of his father, followed shortly thereafter by the loss of Lady Beatrice. I know he discovered that financial matters at the manor were extremely troubling, and it took quite a spell for us to sort everything out. At one point we thought we might have to sell the estate."

"Hadn't you told him of the inheritance you received when you turned twenty-one?" Roderick asked.

"I did finally," she answered. "As I watched him struggle with worry about debt, I couldn't bear keeping secret the fact that I had a great deal of money stashed away in a London bank. It would have been cruel of me not to help him hold fast to Winthrop Manor and its staff. He'd always led such an unencumbered existence—had never faced that sort of difficulty. We were looking at the possibility of total ruin, so I stepped in and helped solve the problem."

"You did the right thing, my dear. Win had a wonderful life as a youngster and on into the years after he became a viscount. Most everything he dreamed of or wished for was his."

"I bailed us out rather quickly, Uncle."

"I understand, Josephine. I'm glad you were honest with him. Perhaps I gave you poor advice when I told you of my belief that a wife should have her own stash of funds and that she bore no obligation to share such information with her husband."

Josephine took a sip of tea. She sat on the sofa in the small parlour, uneasy and deeply anxious.

"The truth about your financial situation has been remedied," Roderick said. "I know Win. Actually, I wouldn't have been completely surprised if he had refused your help. He's an extremely proud man. I'm not at all certain he would have wanted you to solve financial difficulties associated with Winthrop Manor. Nonetheless, I'm glad you confessed everything. It isn't as though you'd only been married a short time. Enough years have passed, and it was time for everything to be out in the open between you."

Josephine reached up and tucked a strand of hair back into the up-do she always wore. "I agree, Uncle. I'm glad we had the chance to discuss it. However, that still leaves my present dilemma. I've never been the sort of wife who badgers her husband. I haven't tried to set boundaries for Win, nor has he with me. But I simply cannot live anymore with his gallivanting off to London night after night. I can't believe he's cheating on me. Well, at least, I don't *think* he is. I've always felt that Win has very high morals. Only, he's never home with me at night. We have our evening meal, and he departs for London, saying he has a meeting or some such nonsense. I know it isn't true. I've been told by others that he can be found night after night at The Pussy Cat Club. I'm sure you've heard of it."

"Oh, yes. Who hasn't? It's apparently where the new breed of young people congregates. Flappers. Isn't that the word for the young ladies?"

"Yes. Win is much too old for such foolishness. He has me and Andy. To be honest, I would love to have another child. The chances of that are slim, however, since he sleeps at the townhouse in Mayfair more often than he does Winthrop Manor."

"You need to have a talk with him, Josephine. You've always had a tendency to let things ride, assuming they'll pass of their own accord."

"Yes. You're right. I'll have to give some thought as to how and when to best approach him, but I shall pour out all my feelings. This isn't a healthy way to live. I've always loved Win with my entire being. I shouldn't hold back my feelings now. He *has* to know he's hurting and confusing me. Also, Andy is growing up. I should think Win would want to spend time with his son."

It was nearing five o'clock when she rang David Carlisle to collect her. She gathered her gloves and pocket book, making ready to depart.

"Thank you, Uncle. You always give the best advice. I love you so and am grateful I have you to discuss things like this." They hugged and kissed goodbye.

Home again, Josephine sat in the drawing room. She'd reached an important decision. Life couldn't continue in such a vein. Her discussion with Uncle Roderick had helped immensely. She'd always been a loving, understanding wife and, even in this instance, she had fine instincts about the reasons for his behaviour. Nevertheless, it had to stop.

With her mind firmly made up, she left the room and hurried up the winding staircase to her bedchamber, where she encountered Emma, her lady's maid.

"Hello, Emma. I'm happy to see you." Josephine smiled. "I need you to help me select a truly elegant gown for this evening."

"Is it a celebration of some sort, milady?" Emma asked.

"No. Not at all. I simply fancy a special night. Following the evening meal, I'm going to do something rather out of character for me." Josephine smiled again, adding a small giggle.

"What on Earth?" asked Emma.

"For quite some time, Win has been returning to London and spending his evenings there, staying in the Mayfair Townhouse, only to return the next day or evening. I've been told by numerous acquaintances that he's often seen at that new club—The Pussy Cat. I intend to pay a visit to the place and see with my own eyes just what intrigues him so much."

Emma covered her mouth with her hand. "Oh, milady, do you think that's wise? Is there the chance that his Lordship will think you don't trust him?"

"Yes, of course, but I'm willing to take such a chance. I'm afraid he's given me reason to doubt him. I need to know what is pulling him toward that club, night after night. Therefore, Emma, I must look resplendent."

"You always look resplendent, if I do say so. Nevertheless, we'll choose the most exceptional frock in your wardrobe," answered Emma.

Together they began to inspect each gown hanging in the large cupboard, which dominated nearly one wall of Josephine's room. She had a plethora of magnificent dresses. However, what she had in mind for that particular evening needed to be uncommonly lovely, and one her husband hadn't seen for a long while, if ever. Often, she purchased gowns she found appealing, so she would have one when an unexpected event presented itself. This was one of those times.

The Victorian style that had ruled during the beginning of the twentieth century called for items like bustles and corsets to literally hold women into the formal, stiff dresses. This was turned completely on its ear by 1920 when frocks became more loose-fitting, with waists that dropped lower and lower. By then, the typical waist was around the hips. Boyish bodies were in vogue for women, and the new styles needed no restricting undergarments in the tube-like dresses. Women had taken to wearing pants and men's dress shirts as well, which was another comfortable style. Dresses were frilly and fringed to go along with short, bobbed hair. Hemlines finally settled just below the knee. Evening dresses had a hemline anywhere from mid-calf to floor length.

Josephine was by no means a flapper, nor did the current fashions delight her. She had a lovely silhouette, and it was the exact opposite of boyish. However, she thought she remembered having purchased a rather daring gown with a bare back, and then hadn't had the cheek to wear it.

Thumbing through her wardrobe, she came upon the frock she'd forgotten having purchased. It was a Madame Vionnet, and she'd bought it in Paris when she and Win had paid a visit to the beautiful City of Lights the previous year. The dress was pale-pink chiffon with a beaded halter, bare-backed top. It was rather scandalous. Josephine had never worn anything so revealing. The front, which dipped into quite a deep V, was also beaded. She knew the moment she saw it again that it was the perfect dress for the night's outing.

Because of the ornate beading on the bodice and back, she chose to wear no jewelry, other than her wedding ring and a high, Cleopatra-style bracelet, which was all the rage. Hers was set with pink diamonds.

Emma agreed the dress was divine. "Why, milady, I don't recall seeing this before. Have you ever worn it? It looks absolutely brand-new."

"No, Emma, I haven't. I fell in love with it, but when we returned to England, I decided it was a bit risqué for me. Still, we'll be going to London this evening, and from what I hear of this Pussy Cat Club, this gown will be perfect. I'm still not certain I won't feel a bit naughty in it, but I think Win will consider it enchanting."

Emma ran a bath, and piled Josephine's thick, chestnut hair on top of her head. After she stepped out of the tub, Josephine slipped into a white, silk robe. Emma unpinned her hair and brushed it until it shined. She still wore it quite long – near her shoulders. She had been contemplating having it cut into one of the new bobs that were seen on every street corner but still wasn't certain she wanted to do away with the locks she'd worn since she was a young girl.

Emma had been urging her to try the new style. "Milady, it will always grow back. I think it would look so chic with your features. Won't you allow me to cut it?"

Emma was an excellent hair stylist. If Josephine were to allow anyone to cut her locks it would be her lady's maid.

"Well, do you truly think it would look all right? I haven't cut my hair since before Win and I married. What if he loathes it?"

"If I thought there was a remote possibility of that, I wouldn't suggest it. Let's give it a go."

"All right, Emma. I hope I don't regret this, but I *am* in the mood for a change." Her hands trembled with fear and trepidation.

Emma snipped and combed with unparalleled concentration.

Josephine was terrified to look into the mirror. Slowly, she turned her body 'round and stared at her reflection. She loved it! She simply adored it! She hadn't worn her hair so short since she was a small child, so it was truly shocking. But the length accentuated her eyes and drew attention to every one of her fine features. Because her hair had natural wave, Emma arranged it so that it curved a bit around her forehead falling into a chin-length bob, curving towards her cheeks. It was incredible that a simple hairstyle could make such a difference in one's appearance.

"Oh, Emma! I *do* think this was a wise choice. I look ages younger. I'd be immensely surprised if Win isn't very much in favour of this. Bless you for convincing me to take the chance. Win should be returning within the hour. My fondest hope is that after tonight, when he sees me enter The Pussy Cat Club, he'll see that his wife is far superior to the Bright Young Things one reads about in the *Times*. Perhaps then he'll resume his usual pattern of staying here at the manor, instead of running off to London."

"I'm certain your hope will be realized." Emma put away all of the various instruments she'd used to transform Josephine's image. Then Emma held the spectacular gown so it could easily slip over her mistress's head.

Once clad in the shell-pink frock, Josephine walked to the cheval mirror. She looked spellbinding. "Emma! Oh, Emma! I look so…I look like a different person. Oh, Lord. I *am* a bit afraid that Win will be dismayed at such a complete makeover."

"Oh, milady, I shouldn't think so. Most men are delighted to see their wives keep up with the times. Surely Lord Winthrop is no different."

"No, I don't believe he is." Josephine smiled and turned this way and that, observing her reflection from all angles. "He should be home soon. I'm really most excited, but a bit nervous."

Emma deposited the wet towels and clothing Josephine had previously worn into a pile to be cleaned and returned to the countess's suite. "Do you wish for me to do any additional makeup, milady?" she asked.

Josephine furrowed her brow and thought for a moment. "Yes. You know I think this new look calls for a bit more glamour. Not *too* much. However, perhaps a change in lip colour—not scarlet red, but a more outstanding shade of darker pink. Also, perhaps my cheeks need additional highlighting with some rouge—certainly, not too much though."

"I agree, milady. Also, how would you feel if I added a bit more charcoal to your lashes? You have such spectacular eyes, and this new hairstyle accentuates them."

"Yes, Emma, I agree. Let's give it a go," Josephine said, laughing.

4

❦

She heard the Rolls Royce on the manor's gravelled drive. Glancing in the great hall's mirror, she moved toward the entryway to greet Win when he came through the doors. He'd stayed in London the night before, so she was anxious to see him and to have their long-awaited conversation.

As he entered the house, she smiled sweetly and put her arms 'round him.

"Hello, darling. I'm so glad you're home. I hate it when you stay in London overnight. Let's have a drink and sit down in the drawing room. I've asked Radcliffe to build a lovely fire in there. It's so cosy," she exclaimed.

Win looked tired. He was either suffering from sleep deprivation or had a bad hangover—possibly both. He returned her hug with a peck on the cheek. "I'm rather worn out, dear. I had meetings that lasted far into the night and more today with bankers. I think I'd rather not have a drink. I'm going to have a wash and a short lie-down. Then I'll change into a fresh suit. We'll dine, and I'll return to London, as I have more meetings early in the morning."

Josephine's heart sank. Her usual reaction would have been to allow Win to climb the stairway without uttering a complaint. However, this routine had gone on for much too long. She took a deep breath and began to speak.

"No. That simply won't do. I'm truly sorry you're tired, but we need to have a serious conversation. This is becoming the norm for you. I'm at my wit's end not knowing how to cope with your behaviour."

"I haven't the faintest notion what you're talking about, Josephine." He looked confused.

"Please, Win." She ran her hand through her newly bobbed hair, feeling hurt that he hadn't noticed. "I think you know precisely what I'm talking about. You haven't spent an evening, let alone a *night*, with me in a very long time. Do you think I'm ignorant? I don't believe you have business dealings in London every night. You know I'm right."

"Are you accusing me of not telling you the truth?"

"Yes. While I hate to admit it, that is exactly what I'm doing. I'm not stupid. I am sick and tired of your foolish excuses to spend nights in London. I read the *London Times*, you know. Aren't you aware that the names of people who frequent The Pussy Cat Club are printed in the society pages?"

A stunned look crossed her husband's face, as if that fact had never crossed his mind. He was silent for a moment and then quickly changed the subject.

"Darling, you've bobbed your hair. Forgive me for not noticing the moment I entered the house. Turn around... let me see the back," he urged.

Josephine acquiesced to his wishes, but she wasn't about to allow him to change the subject.

"Oh, I *do* like it. Quite. Of course, you're always beautiful, but this new hairdo makes you look years younger."

"Really? I imagine you're quite used to this new trend on all of the Bright Young Things you spend time with at The Pussy Cat Club."

"Josephine, *please*. You know I've never looked at another woman since I met you." His face had taken on a pale shade. It was apparent that he realized he was not going to wrangle his way out of the fix he found himself in.

"Win, I ran into an old school chum of mine in Winthrop-on-Hart today. Her name is Barbara Stanley. She told me she recently spotted you leaving The Pussy Cat Club early in the morning hours with a young girl dressed as a flapper. Is *she* what fascinates you so about nightlife in London?"

He reached out his hand and took hold of hers. "Let's sit down. You're right, as usual. I need to make a clean breast of things." He led her to the sofa in front of the large drawing room fireplace, and they sat.

Radcliffe appeared, bearing two glasses of gin and tonic.

"I'll not lie to you. I never thought I would resort to subterfuge, and it's time I tell you the entire truth."

"What is it? Is there a problem?"

"I suppose you could say so," he replied. "You see, I *have* been going to The Pussy Cat Club. The first time I visited there, I had no of intention of staying. I dropped by because I'd heard of its opening and was curious. When I entered the club, I was totally astounded, since it's much more glamorous than I'd anticipated. I saw several of the chaps who attended Oxford with me, and they invited me to have a drink with them. I figured I'd have one quick drink and head back to Winthrop Manor. Then, one of my chums suggested a game of poker. Actually, as you know, I've never been keen about the game, but found myself agreeing to play a hand or two." Win turned to look at his wife.

"Yes, however," she retorted. "You *didn't* win, you *lost*. Am I correct?"

He hung his head and ran a hand through his thick, black hair. "Yes, you're right. Oh, I *did* win some...enough to keep me going. Eventually, I lost the entire twenty thousand."

Josephine jumped to her feet. Never in the course of their marriage had she displayed such anger. How could her husband be so foolish? She pulled a face and glared at him. "All right, Win. Just exactly how far in debt are we?"

"Oh, God, Josephine. I hate to tell you. It's very bad. Not only did I lose the original twenty thousand, but I lost over fifty thousand pounds more."

"God's nightgown, Win! How could you? I'm terribly angry. You're not a stupid man. You have always shown good sense and high morals. Now, you'll ride off on Black Orchid, leaving me to come up with a solution. There will be taxes due on Winthrop Manor soon and on the London house, not to mention Andy's schooling. Eton will follow in no time at all. Have you any idea how much Eton costs? We gave all of the staff wage raises when I managed to bail us out with my inheritance. What are we to do now?"

Win stood and attempted to put his arms 'round Josephine, but she pulled away from him and walked across the drawing room. "You still haven't told me the identity of the woman Barbara saw with you. Barbara said you had your arm about her waist, assisting her into the Rolls Royce. Who is she?"

"Oh, she's nobody important—just someone I know who'd had a bit too much to drink. I offered her a ride home since she doesn't live far from our townhouse. I intended to put her into a taxicab but couldn't find one that was empty. So I gave up. It just seemed easier and quicker to allow David to drive us both."

"What if someone who knows us had seen you? What conclusion do you think they would have drawn? In fact, Barbara Stanley *did* see you."

"I apologise, Josephine. I didn't think of that. You have to know I've never so much as looked at another woman since I met you."

"There was a time I would have believed that, but I'm not so certain now. You have been acting so odd. Barbara also said she saw you lean over and kiss this unknown woman once you were both in the car. Perhaps you're having an affaire with her."

"Darling! Never! I was simply being kind."

"It most surely would have been more kind had you been home in your own bed with me," she replied. "I'd suggest you start this confession over again."

"Josephine, I *did*, indeed, kiss her. She was quite drunk, babbling on about how she was in love with me and had been since first setting eyes upon me. I simply gave her a small kiss on the cheek to stop such nonsensical talk."

"The only way I feel I can regain my trust in you is if you're willing for me to meet this 'flapper' Barbara saw with you. What is her name and where does she live? How old is she?"

"Her name is Fiona Porter. I don't know where she lives permanently. Her family has leased a temporary home in Mayfair for the Season. She's only eighteen—just a silly, young girl."

Josephine had been pacing up and down the room, her head down, listening to his explanation. She whirled about.

"Eighteen! My God, Win. What in the world is wrong with you?"

He pulled a face. "If you had agreed to accompany me to The Pussy Cat Club, this wouldn't have happened. You would have made certain I didn't do anything foolish. I know I should have walked away when I won at poker, but I had a desire to play just one more hand. I also shouldn't have cared about how Fiona made it back to her home."

"No, but instead you chose to take an eighteen-year-old debutante home. *Did* you go straight to her home?" She shook her head, thoroughly disgusted. "This isn't the way you used to be. You were always so sensible. I can't imagine what's gotten into you. I don't know how I'm supposed to cope with this. Look what a mess our lives have become. We're in a terrible amount of trouble financially. I have a strong suspicion you're involved with a girl young enough to be your daughter while I spend night after night alone. Andy scarcely knows you any more—this is a bloody nightmare!"

"Darling, please calm down. You're letting your imagination run away with you," Win pleaded. "Not to mention the fact that *you* are always telling me not to curse, and I believe you just said 'bloody.'"

"I'll calm down when all of this is sorted out. To begin with, *yes*, I am going to accompany you to The Pussy Cat Club tonight."

His face blanched. He obviously had never dreamed she would agree to go. "Oh, darling, I'm really not at all certain you would enjoy it very much. It's primarily a men's club, you know."

"*Really, Win*. From what I heard from Barbara Stanley, there are quite a few flapper-type women emerging from the club night after night."

"There are undoubtedly some. There always are. I'm just not sure you'd enjoy their sort."

"Let me be the judge of that. In the meantime, you can devote your time to trying to figure a solution to the god-awful nightmare we're in financially."

"Why don't we ask your Uncle Roderick for some help? You know he has thousands of acres of land. He could solve our difficulties in a heartbeat."

"I cannot believe you would even suggest such a thing. This is not Uncle Roderick's problem. I have the solution. We're going to sell the London townhouse. If necessary, we'll also sell the cottage you built for me to live in while you were away at war."

"I refuse to consider doing either of those things," Win answered. "We aren't destitute. There has to be a better way to settle the debts."

"Well, tell me what it is then," Josephine demanded in a sarcastic voice.

"I need some time to think. I'm not the only chap who's found himself in this sort of dilemma."

"Well, you can keep thinking of a solution while I'm enjoying a night out at The Pussy Cat Club, "Josephine snapped back.

Win slumped down on the sofa. "Oh, Josephine. I'm sorry. I know what I did was ridiculous. I need your help, darling. I'm not certain it's a good idea for you to accompany me to the club."

"I'm going with you. I don't want to hear any more of your foolish arguments. You had the cheek to place the blame on *me* for your ridiculous loss of money, and I intend to show you that I have nothing to do with the mess you've created. I'm completely undone by this news. I bailed us out after the war, when the economy hit rock bottom. My inheritance is *gone*. What in the world were you thinking

"Josephine, I didn't mean what I said. I'm totally aware that I made a dreadful mistake in judgment. You know I've never been this sort of person. I can't explain why I've been acting like such a fool. All I can promise is that I intend to stop."

"We'll start by accompanying me to this den of iniquity where you've been spending *far too many* nights. I think it's high time I got a look at it for myself."

A shadow of fear came over Win's face. "Do you promise you'll not become angry with me if there are people present who appear to know me well?"

"Yes, Win. I promise. However, I'm a bit confused. If all you've been doing is playing cards with other chaps, I don't know why you seem overly concerned that I might be upset at friends who recognise you. Are you implying that these friends are *women*?"

"Well, of course I've met some women who hang about the club. The place is very congenial."

"Have you been enjoying yourself with some of these Bright Young Things, as the *London Times* describes them?"

"What if I have? I can assure you I've done nothing untoward. Perhaps I've bought a drink or two or had a dance."

"I suppose I'll be given an opportunity to meet these new friends," she retorted. "Now, let me pack a few items. I assume we'll be staying at the Mayfair house?"

He looked as though he'd been placed into a trap and wondered how he got there. "Yes, of course, we'll go to Curzon Street. Unless, of course, you'd rather spend the night at Claridges or the Savoy?"

"That seems rather silly." Josephine smiled. "When we own a house in Mayfair, why spend money on a posh hotel?"

"Yes, you're right. We'll dine here, and then drive back to London after we eat."

She began to walk toward the stairway then turned and faced him. "No. We'll dine in London. I want to be on our way. I'm going to pack an overnight case. David will drive us, I assume? Will he stay in the rooms over the garages in Mayfair?"

"Yes. That's the usual arrangement." Win looked uncomfortable

She was as angry and as disappointed in Win as she'd ever dreamed possible. As she ascended the staircase, Win turned and left the drawing room, heading in the direction of the library.

Win heard his wife descend the staircase less than a half hour later. Then the door opened. David Carlisle must have taken her bag and stowed it in the boot of the auto. He did not hear Andy's footsteps, so he must have been in his own room. Win picked himself up from the armchair by the fireplace. He put his face in his hands, and tried to stifle tears he knew were about to begin.

He had *not* been completely honest with his wife. The truth wasn't devastating, but he wasn't certain she'd believe him. Perhaps he'd be fortunate and she wouldn't learn of his stupidity. Hopefully, Fiona Porter wouldn't be at The Pussy Cat Club tonight. The silly girl never knew when to keep her mouth shut.

What had begun as grief and anxiety was turning to anger. There were scores of married men at the Pussy Cat every night. His presence was no different than the others. Since when did Josephine think she was going to organise his social-life for him?

He strode across the drawing room and took the stairs two at a time. When he reached Andy's room, he stopped outside of the door and listened. No sound came from within. Slowly, he turned the doorknob. His son was sleeping soundly with his arm tucked about his little terrier, Twist. The nanny was also asleep in the adjoining bed chamber. Now that Andy had turned ten and would be attending school at the Winfield Academy the following autumn, the nanny would be leaving. She'd already lined up another position.

Yes. Fine. He'd have David run them up to London. He continued on to his own bed chamber and changed his clothing to a dinner jacket ensemble. He slid a couple of clean shirts and trousers into an overnight valise. By the time he'd finished, he heard the Rolls engine roaring outside the entrance to the manor. Win zipped the bag shut and scurried down the steps. As David entered the front doorway, he told the driver of their plans. "Wait just a moment, David. I want to tell Mrs. Shellady where Josephine and I have gone so she will know how to reach us, if need be."

"Right, milord," answered David.

Win found her in the kitchen, sitting at the long table that served as the dining area for the staff's meal. She was sipping a cup of tea with Mrs. Boyle, the head cook who had replaced Mrs. Whitaker. Mrs. Vera Whitaker had been with the family for decades but was suffering from dementia. She'd been kept on at the manor as a loyal retainer, with her own suite of rooms.

"Both Lady Josephine and I are going to be out this evening. We'll be staying at the house in Mayfair. If you need either of us, you know where we can be reached," Win added.

"Yes, milord," answered the housekeeper. "But aren't you going to eat your evening meal?"

"No. We'll dine in London."

"All right, milord. Don't worry about anything here. I'll keep a close eye on Andy."

"Thank you, Mrs. Shellady," Win replied. "We'll see you sometime tomorrow."

Win met up with David in the great hall. "Got Lady Josephine settled, have you?" Win asked.

"Quite, sir," his long-time driver answered. "Sir, I'm ready whenever you are."

"Right. Well, I hate to inform you that we want you to drive back to London now."

The two men left the house, and while David slid behind the steering mechanism, Win settled next to his wife on the soft, leather seat in the back of the Rolls. "The Pussy Cat Club then," he instructed David.

Josephine did not look pleased.

5

༄

Josephine and Win arrived at The Pussy Cat Club a bit after nine o'clock in the evening. The place was already filled with a truly amazing conglomeration of clientele. Josephine was stunned. There were, indeed, many gentlemen, but she would have estimated she saw an equal number of females. However, they were attired like no women she had ever known. "I find it difficult to believe that these are women who are accepted in polite society," she whispered to Win.

"Oh, sweetheart, it's just the way the younger generation present themselves. Look, even you have resorted to bobbing your hair in order to make yourself appear more modern. Generations change."

"The problem is that we are not of *their* generation. We do not belong with *this* crowd."

"Well, we're here now, so let's have a cocktail and relax," he answered in a rather exasperated tone.

The room was designed in the style of a gentleman's library, with hunting prints on the walls and bookcases overflowing with classics. There were a few tables and a good-sized dance floor, but also comfy sofas scattered about.

"I would really prefer to sit on a sofa, if you're in agreement." Josephine looked around the room.

"Oh, but darling, wouldn't you like to join a few others? It's so much more congenial to sit at a table and converse with new friends."

"I don't mean to be critical, but I truly don't see anyone I want to meet or chat with."

Before they had a chance to continue the conversation, a young lady with flaming red hair, dressed in a green silk dress fringed at the bottom and cut above her knees, came rushing over to Win.

"Win, you wonderful man! How marvellous to see you here again tonight," she gushed. She couldn't have reached the age of twenty yet.

Josephine was appalled.

"Hello, Fiona." Win looked chagrined. His hopes that Fiona wouldn't be present were dashed. He turned to his wife. "Fiona, may I present my wife, the Countess of Winthrop, Lady Josephine," he stated.

"How lovely to meet you, Countess." The young lady dipped into a curtsy.

Josephine extended her gloved hand, but Fiona ignored it. She was obviously too enamoured with Win, trying to persuade him to join the table she was sharing with several other debutantes and their escorts. It was clear to Josephine that *her own* wishes were to be overridden, when Win smiled broadly and agreed to Fiona's invitation.

The three made their way to a round table, almost directly in the middle of the room. Josephine hadn't the slightest desire to be the center of attention, and glanced longingly back at the quiet sofa she'd been eyeing before Fiona's interruption.

When they arrived at the table, both she and Win were introduced to the others. All the ladies were dressed similar to Fiona. There was an enormous fuss made about Win. Almost as an afterthought, Josephine was introduced to the others. Then, after placing a drink order, she was ignored.

Josephine could think of nothing whatsoever to converse with them about anyway. All were nearly an entire generation behind her and her husband, and there was nothing she could possibly imagine having in common with them. When the band began to play a tune that Josephine had never heard and didn't particularly care for, Fiona leaned over and asked whether she minded if Win danced with her. There was little she could do, but tell the young lady that it would be fine.

To her amazement, Win took to the floor and did the Charleston, which utterly amazed Josephine. She had no idea her husband was so proficient in modern dance.

Drinks continued to be served, and by the end of the evening, the majority of the guests were not sober. Josephine had never been fond of alcohol and had consumed only two glasses of white wine. The others were drinking exotic drinks she'd never heard of with names like Manhattans, Black Russians, Dirty Martinis, and Orange Blossoms.

Finally, it was time to depart, and it could not have come a moment too quickly for Josephine. Fiona was tagging along behind her, obviously having drunk far too many of the odd drinks. She even planted a kiss on Win's cheek, begging him to stay longer, but to his credit, he *did* refuse.

Then, just as they were about to exit the club, Fiona looked at Josephine. "Oh, Lady Winthrop, I forgot to thank you for allowing Win to lend me your beautiful—"

Win quickly interrupted. "Yes, Fiona. Josephine was happy to do so. We must be going now."

Josephine looked puzzled. What was the little fool referring to? Josephine had never met her before, so how could she possibly have loaned her anything? Perhaps she was speaking of the night Win had asked David to drive to her home. Was she thanking Josephine for lending her the Rolls Royce? This was one more thing she needed to speak to Win about.

They made their way to the automobile, where David was waiting patiently. She was tired, had the beginnings of a headache, and simply wanted to put her head on a pillow.

Win seemed a bit out of sorts, undoubtedly because she had not been particularly friendly, never joining in the revelry. They spoke little on the drive to the townhouse in Mayfair. Upon arrival, he took out the key, opened the door, and escorted her into the pleasant home. They *did* have a maid on the premises, but Win had not expected her to stay up into the wee hours simply to open the door.

Josephine immediately headed for the master bedroom. They had a local lady come to clean the home once a week, so everything was neat as a pin and smelled like beeswax. She set her valise down inside the bedroom, went to the bath area and poured herself a glass of cold water, bringing it to the side table by the bed. She quickly undressed, hanging the stunning pink gown in the cupboard. Then she opened a drawer in the dresser and plucked out a lovely, white Queen Anne's Lace cotton nightgown and maneuvered it over her head. She drew back the white duvet cover on the bed, exposing the lovely, crisp sheets.

Something pink slid from beneath them. Her heart felt as though it skipped a beat. She stared at the bed, stunned. A pair of pink, women's knickers had attached themselves to the underside of the sheets. They were definitely *not hers.* They were the sort of undergarment that a younger woman would wear. Tears streamed down her cheeks. She couldn't catch her breath. It was absolutely clear that Win had brought another woman into *their* bed. The site of the pink underwear changed everything. *How could he? He had been lying about everything he'd said only a few hours ago.*

Well, not everything. She believed his recitation of the trouble he was in due to his obsession with poker. However, the tale he'd told about Fiona had been total fabrication. Josephine would have bet her last pound that the feminine undergarment on her bed belonged to the same lady she had met earlier whom he'd supposedly driven home. She had a rather awful feeling that the two had driven to the townhouse and spent the night making passionate love in the bed that only she and Win had ever occupied.

Crying hysterically, she ran to the hallway just as Win was climbing the last step to the bedroom floor.

"Win, how could you? I cannot believe you would betray me like this. I'm just all undone. I have to get out of here. I refuse to spend a night with a scoundrel. Was it Fiona?"

"What in the world are you speaking about?" Win looked genuinely puzzled.

"Win, when I pulled back the sheets, ready to crawl into bed, a pair of pink, woman's knickers were laying there. Now, don't try to deny that there wasn't a woman in that bed."

She turned and ran down the stairs to the front doorway.

Win followed. "No, Josephine, you have it all wrong. At least give me time to explain."

"There is nothing to explain. You have clearly betrayed me with another woman. Most probably that dreadful Fiona. There is nothing you can say to convince me differently. I never want to see you again. I shall see a solicitor tomorrow and file for a decree of divorce on the grounds of adultery."

She opened the front door and ran outside. Half-crazed with anger and grief, she paid no attention to where she was going. She ran straight onto Curzon Street.

Win followed, greatly upset as well. They were standing in the middle of the street when a car, driving at a higher-than-usual rate of speed, hit them square on. Both were thrown into the air and landed on the street with a sickening thud.

A lady who lived in a townhouse on the other side of Curzon Street heard the noise. She pulled her draperies and was astonished to observe the scene. It was wretched. She threw on robe and slippers, stopped at the telephone in the foyer and rang for an ambulance. She then proceeded to see if she could render any assistance. When she reached them, the gentleman appeared to be dead. He was dressed in evening wear. She felt for a pulse, but could find none.

She turned her attention to the lady, who was wearing a lovely white nightdress. The woman was moaning and tears were streaming down her face. Blood was everywhere. It was clear that she was severely injured, but if the ambulance arrived quickly enough, perhaps with medical attention, she would survive. The woman held Josephine's hand, smoothing her hair back and murmured encouraging words. At long last, she heard sirens in the distance.

The vehicle pulled up and parked near the curb. Two men in white uniforms rushed to Josephine and Win. Each man concerned himself with one of the pair, but Win was beyond help. Thus, the man moved on to Josephine, assisting his partner in making a cursory examination. She was clearly in terrible pain, and one of the attendants administered an injection of morphine. They suspected she could have internal bleeding in addition to the blood pouring from a terrible gash on her thigh and an arm that could well be broken.

With great care, Josephine was lifted onto a gurney and placed into the ambulance. One of the men returned to Win's body and searched his pockets. There he found a wallet with an identification card. The heavy vellum card showed that he held the title, Earl of Winthrop, and that his primary address was Winthrop Manor in Hampshire. A telephone number was also printed at the bottom. One of the attendants radioed for a second vehicle in which Win's body would be transported to the London morgue. Both attendants jumped behind the wheel, turned the siren on again and headed for St Bartholomew's Hospital.

When a call was placed to Winthrop Manor, it was Mrs. Shellady who answered. She could not imagine who would be ringing at such an ungodly hour. When she received the news, she was overcome with grief, but as any proper English servant would do, she held her chin high, wiped her eyes on her sleeve, and proceeded to place a call to Win's sister, Elisabeth Drew.

Elisabeth was devastated. She and Tom rushed to London to be at Josephine's bedside. When they arrived, she was in surgery. They waited for what seemed hours, and finally the physician who'd performed surgery approached them in the waiting area.

"Oh, doctor," cried Elisabeth. "What is Josephine's condition?"

"She should recover without any lasting effects," he answered with a smile. "She has a broken arm, but to my great relief, she has no internal injuries, which is extremely fortunate. She has also suffered a concussion, but it's mild and I expect no after effects. There will be a scar on her upper leg, but I believe it can be taken care of with good reconstructive surgery if need be. She is still in the recovery area, but you will be able to see her within an hour, or so. All in all, she came through such a dastardly accident in quite decent shape. It's terrible that she apparently lost her husband in the same incident. She will have to be told, of course, but I would wait a few days to make certain she's ready for such shocking news."

Elisabeth and Tom nodded their heads in agreement. With that, the physician left the waiting area. The couple continued to sit, in anticipation of permission to see Josephine. Finally, they were advised to follow a nurse. When they entered the hospital room, they could see that Josephine's left arm was in a plaster cast and her leg had a bandage covering it. She still seemed somewhat drowsy as a result of the anesthesia that had been administered. Both Tom and Elisabeth leaned down and kissed her, saying how extremely happy they were that she was going to be all right. Josephine smiled feebly, taking Elisabeth's hand into her own. Slurring her words, a bit, she enquired about her husband's condition.

"Josephine, let's talk about Win when you're feeling a little better." Elisabeth's eyes were still red and swollen from tears she'd shed over the loss of her beloved brother.

"No, Elisabeth. I need to know now or I won't be able to rest. Please, tell me how Win is," she implored.

Elisabeth looked to her husband, not knowing quite how to proceed. He *was,* after all, a physician himself, albeit a country doctor.

Tom nodded his head affirmatively.

"Oh, my dear," Elisabeth began. "It seems that tragedy follows you throughout life. It shatters me to have to tell you that Win lost his life in this terrible mishap."

Josephine buried her head in the pillow and sobbed. "Oh my God! This is my fault. I've literally caused my husband's death. I accused him of cheating on me. Neither of us would have been in the center of that street if I hadn't run from Win, making vile accusations."

"Whatever are you talking about?" asked Elisabeth.

Josephine managed to relate the story of what had occurred in the townhouse.

Elisabeth was stunned. "Oh, surely you were wrong, Josephine. I cannot believe that Win would ever have betrayed you. He loved you so dearly. However, please darling, don't blame yourself," she added. "We'll discuss this more when you've rested."

"Yes, but I must plan funeral services for Win. I refuse to allow anyone else to take over a task that should be mine."

"We understand, dearest," Elisabeth answered. "However, right now, you need rest. You've had a terrible shock. Try to rest, and we'll discuss this further tomorrow."

"Where is Win now?" she asked.

"At the London morgue," her sister-in-law replied. "They require an autopsy in a situation like this. Therefore, it will be several days before any sort of service can be arranged."

Four days later, Josephine was discharged from hospital and David collected her, driving her to Winthrop Manor. Upon arrival, all of the staff came rushing out of the mansion, eager to see their mistress and to shower her with affection and love. Of course, the first to place their arms about her was Andrew, her dear son, who was now the Earl of Winthrop. "Oh, Mummy," he sobbed. "Is it true? Is Daddy dead?"

"Yes, darling," she replied. "I shall need you more than ever, Andy. However, I don't wish for this to alter your plans to attend school in the autumn. Your father would be most disappointed if you didn't carry through on the arrangement he and I made for your future. Your education is now more important than ever, for you will assume the duties of the earl once you reach the age of majority. Come, Andy. Let's go into the house. I know this has been a terrible shock, but we all must keep a stiff upper lip. I *do* understand how you feel. I lost both of my parents at about the same age. I know I can never replace your father, but I shall make every effort to be the best mother a young man could have."

"You always have been," he cried. "I'll do whatever you ask of me. But I wish I could stay here to watch over you. I am now the man of the house."

"Yes, dear. Nevertheless, I *am* still your guardian until you turn twenty-one. You must trust that I know what is best."

"Yes, I shall," he answered, his expression sorrowful.

Josephine made an attempt to smile. "Good. Now, the first order of business will be to make plans for your father's burial."

Andy looked devastated, but didn't cry. "Where will that be?" he asked.

"We shall have services in the Winthrop Manor chapel, of course, and then he will be laid to rest in the family mausoleum outside of the chapel in the cemetery. He will lie next to his mother and father, as you and I will someday. We'll all be reunited in heaven." She valiantly smiled.

"That's a nice thought." Andy continued to look downward, holding his emotions tightly locked inside of his ten-year-old body.

6

***

Josephine—her arm still in plaster with a smaller dressing on her leg—her lovely chestnut hair stunning it its newly cut bob, appeared at Win's service looking serene, though mournful. It was important to her that she present herself as a composed countess, since in her heart it would be her last gift to the man she had adored. Regardless of what he might have done to break their marriage vows, she refused to hold on to anger. She forgave him any transgressions, placing the blame for any such action upon his frightful experiences during the Great War.

She had been paid a call by a gentleman named Nigel French, who was a frequent visitor to The Pussy Cat Club and had many times played that wretched poker with Win. When he first introduced himself, she thought he was an odious man, wanting to collect on Win's large gambling debts before his body was even interred.

However, Mr. French had paid the call to inform her that all of the men Win had been involved with in poker games had joined together and signed a petition stating that the debts were forgiven. It *was* an enormous relief to Josephine, and she thanked Mr. French profusely. She still planned to put the Mayfair townhouse on the market, but the economy was such that she had scant hope of selling it for its true worth. Still, the house was in a prime location and had been kept in pristine condition, so she *did* expect a better-than-average price.

When the service began, Josephine was escorted to her seat in a front pew by Joseph Haworth, the vicar of St. Luke's Church in Winthrop-on-Hart, who always performed any services that took place in the chapel at Winthrop Manor. She held Andrew's hand in hers, tremendously proud of her handsome young boy who greatly resembled his deceased father. The two sat next to one another, gazing at the casket, which sat at the front of the chapel, covered in a blanket of red roses. Along with Josephine and Andrew, Elisabeth and Tom were seated beside her. Uncle Roderick held her other hand. This was all of the family Win had left, since his brother Oliver was still in prison. Josephine requested that the Winthrop Manor staff be seated in the row directly behind the family, since most had been extremely close to him.

It was an exemplary service. The opening hymn was "Jerusalem," and there wasn't a dry eye in the quaint, old place of worship when the last verse was sung. Following that, there were readings from the Bible by people who had been especially close to Win through the years, including David Carlisle, his chauffeur; Radcliffe, the family butler; and Mrs. Shellady, the housekeeper.

In a somewhat unusual break with tradition, Josephine herself stood and made her way to the podium to give the eulogy. She spoke of meeting Win and went on to recount their great love. No mention was made of the night he'd lost his life.

While standing at the front of the chapel speaking, Josephine looked across the crowd congregated to pay their respects to her husband. She was dumbfounded to see Fiona, the young lady from The Pussy Cat Club, sitting in a pew quite close to the front. It was a tremendously unseemly thing for her to show up on such a day, but Josephine brushed it aside for the moment, making a mental note to speak to the girl after the service had ended. She concluded by saying that, while it was not always an easy task for her to speak in public, she felt the eulogy was to be her last gift to Win.

The entire congregation then took communion at the altar, which is the Church of England way. The hymn, "Amazing Grace," ended the service. Josephine broke down, sobbing. Andrew stood beside her, again telling her that he would always be with her to see that she was loved and cared for.

Following the internment, the many attendees made their way to Winthrop Manor for a lovely funeral luncheon. She kept the vow she'd made to herself, and as she entered the house, she spotted Fiona sipping a glass of wine while carrying a plate of food to a sofa in the drawing room. Josephine walked straight toward her. The girl was dressed appropriately in a smart, black suit with a small hat perched upon her head.

"I don't mean to be rude," Josephine began, "but what on Earth made you think you would be welcomed here today?"

Fiona stood, executing a curtsy, as though Josephine were royalty. "I simply wanted to pay my respects to a fine gentleman who treated me kindly," she replied.

"Yes, I believe I have evidence of the kindness he showed you," Josephine said.

"Whatever do you mean?" Fiona asked.

"A pair of pink knickers were discovered in the bed that Win and I always share when at the townhouse in London. I am certain they must belong to you."

The young lady turned scarlet. "Oh, no, Lady Josephine, you mustn't let such a thought enter your head," she cried. "Yes, they *do* belong to me, but they didn't end up in the bed in the manner you must be thinking. Your husband kindly drove me to his home one evening when I'd consumed far too much alcohol. He was going to take me to my own flat, but I was much too drunk to give him directions. He settled me in his bed, and he slept in another room. I don't *ever* sleep in my knickers. He gave me a lovely nightdress of yours to wear. In fact, I tried to thank you for that gown when you and Win were leaving The Pussy Cat Club the night he died. I was awfully sick that night when we reached the townhouse in Mayfair. He took me upstairs and showed me the bedroom. Honestly, I couldn't have negotiated the stairway without his assistance. I remember slipping out of my knickers after I was under the covers. Nothing happened, Lady Josephine. *Nothing.* I was most grateful for his help. I could very easily have been accosted by any number of ruffians, since I was in such a despicable state. The next morning, he gave me a stern lecture on the dangers of drinking at such a young age and drove me to the nearest tube station. I went home with no knickers, because I didn't know what had become of them. Later that day, I remembered kicking them off in the bed. I was too ashamed to ring him and ask for their return. Anyway, I thought a maid would find them when changing the sheets and probably dispose of them."

Josephine stood absolutely still during the entire recitation. If the story *was* indeed true, there had been no reason for her to have run into Curzon Street or for Win to have chased her. *My God, I am responsible for Win's death!* Tears welled in her eyes. "Thank you," she responded to Fiona. "I'm sorry, but I don't remember your surname."

"My full name is Fiona Porter," she replied. "I'm terribly sorry if I've caused you grief. When I learned of the earl's death, I felt I had to show my respect for him since he was so utterly kind to me. In honour of him, I shall never take another drink of alcohol in my life."

Josephine was aware that Fiona hadn't the slightest notion that *she* had been the direct cause of the uproar that had ended with Win's death. There was certainly no reason to tell her now. Thus, Josephine extended her hand and shook Fiona's. "Thank you for coming and for relating your story to me. Win was a wonderful man and a true gentleman. It would have been like him to do something kind for you."

With that, she turned and made her way through the crowded drawing room, stopping and speaking to other guests along the way. The turnout was so tremendous, Josephine really had no inkling of the name of each person.

She now realised that nearly the entire village of Winthrop-on-Hart was there, as well as those who had known him in London, and even at Ascot.

As she turned to make her way to the kitchen to ask the cook for a glass of iced water, she was brought up short. Oliver, Win's utterly disgusting brother, who had attempted to kidnap little Andy, stood in the corner with an obnoxious sneer on his face.

Anger bubbled up inside. She attempted to maintain her composure and walked to where Oliver stood, sipping a drink. "What in God's name are _you_ doing here?" she asked.

"I was granted compassionate leave to attend my brother's funeral," he retorted. "Don't worry, milady, there is a man from Scotland Yard here too. He's watching my every move. I'll be returned to prison quite soon."

"I should hope so." She was still shocked to see the man she loathed above all others.

"Andy is looking well." Oliver smiled.

"No thanks to you, Oliver. In fact, if you'd had your way, he wouldn't even be here. He would in London and wouldn't know that he was Win's son."

"Yes. Quite true," he said.

"Why don't you leave, Oliver? The funeral service is over. There is no further reason for you to be here. There really was no cause anyway. Win never wanted you to set foot in Winthrop Manor again. You knew that."

"Yes, but Win is no longer with us, is he?" Oliver had the audacity to smile.

Josephine would have liked to slap his face, but instead simply turned her back, walking away from his disgusting presence.

Nonetheless, Oliver had more important things on his mind. He had no intention of returning to the hell-hole known as Wandsworth Prison. He had worked out a perfect scheme, fully intending to carry through with it. Placing his drink on a side table, he approached the guard from Scotland Yard, asking permission to use the lavatory. The guard nodded, but followed Oliver as he left the drawing room.

Oliver had an enormous advantage, however. The guard did not know the floor plan at Winthrop Manor. Oliver did. Instead of using any one of several loos on the second level where he was at the moment, Oliver walked down the stairway to the lower level. He passed through the kitchen, walked down the hall, and entered the water closet meant for staff use. Oliver was well aware that there were _two_ entrances to that loo—one directly off the kitchen, and one which opened onto a hallway.

He entered it from the hallway, quickly closing the door. He had no need for use of the facility. Instead, he rapidly opened the door to the kitchen and exited. The cook, Mrs. Boyle, the under-cook, and several of the other kitchen helpers were scurrying about, attending to the preparation of food for the event. No one even looked up when Oliver hurried through the large room. There was an outside entrance to the kitchen, and he made his way to the doorway, escaping the house.

Without delay, he rushed to the garages, where the family autos were kept. He knew beyond a doubt that David, the chauffeur, would not be there, for he had participated in the service and had also been present in the drawing room. The keys to the cars were hung on pegs in the garages. He quickly plucked the one necessary to operate one of the smaller, less ostentatious vehicles, and slid into the driver's seat.

Moments later, he was speeding down the gravelled drive. His goal was to reach the small cottage that Win had requisitioned for Josephine while he was fighting in the Great War. Oliver certainly knew it well, for that was where he had kidnapped Andy as an infant. He had no intention of staying there very long. It seemed logical that a search would begin upon the Winthrop Manor premises. In fact, it may have already begun. Once that had been accomplished, the very last thing the authorities would imagine was that Oliver would return to Winthrop Manor. He had one more score to settle before escaping to London and beyond.

7

❧❧

Josephine leaned her back against the doorway. I'm terribly grateful for the enormous show of affection. It only proved how much Win was loved and adored by everyone he came into contact with."

"Spot on, Josephine," Tom said. "He was a unique person—one of a kind, really. I shall miss him enormously. Nonetheless, we must carry on. It's what he would want. You need rest, my dear. You are only recently out of hospital. Now, please go to your rooms and have a lie-down. I'll instruct the staff not to bother you until you show your face downstairs again."

"Yes, thank you, Tom. I *am* tired. Aren't you and Elisabeth going to rest as well?"

"Indeed, we are. Just let me have a word with Radcliffe, and we'll be along shortly."

Josephine wearily climbed the staircase. Her head ached, and she was exhausted. When she reached the rooms she'd shared with Win, tears formed. She had been stoic all day, but now it was safe to show the excessive amount of grief she had bottled up inside. She was glad, after all, that Fiona had attended the service. Had she chosen to stay away, Josephine might never have known the truth about her husband's kindness to the young lady.

Would she ever be able to get over the guilt she harboured? There was no doubt in her mind that she was directly responsible for Win's death. He'd begged her to listen, and she'd refused his pleas. Throwing herself across the down-filled comforter on the four-poster bed, she cried until there were simply no more tears to be shed.

❧❧

She woke with a start. How long had she been sleeping? It seemed like hours. She went to the parlour adjoining the bedroom in the master suite and opened the draperies. The sun was setting in the west, and soon darkness would envelop the manor. It had been approximately two o'clock when she'd entered the suite. The lie-down had obviously been needed. She went back to the bedroom, and slipped out of her now-wrinkled clothing. Since it was soon going to be dark outside, she saw no reason to change back into something formal for dinner. She had no intention of following the usual routine for dining at Winthrop Manor. She slipped on a white cotton nightgown with lace at the collar and cuffs and a matching robe. Then she rang the bell for Emma. Shortly, the sweet, young maid appeared.

"Oh, Emma. I can't believe I slept so long. I must have been even more tired than I realised."

"Milady, you've been through one of the worst experiences life can throw at a person. You handled the entire tragedy with poise and dignity. Lord Winthrop would have been exceptionally proud of you."

"Thank you, Emma." Josephine made an attempt at a watery smile. Changing the subject, she asked, "Where is Andy? I know he went out for a ride after the services and the hospitality gathering here at the manor. He *has* returned?"

"Yes, indeed. I saw him come in and go straight to his room. I imagine he's dressing for dinner."

What about Tom and Elisabeth?" Josephine enquired.

"They've taken a short trip over to Cloverdale to retrieve some items. I understand they've decided to stay here for the next few weeks, so you won't be alone."

"Oh dear," replied Josephine. "I sincerely hope I'm not creating difficulty for them. I would be perfectly fine here with my wonderful staff."

"I think they truly want to be with you, milady. Elisabeth, in particular, is grieving the loss of her beloved brother. Being with you comforts her. Do you want me to assist in helping you dress for dinner?" Emma asked.

"Oh no, no, Emma. Just the opposite. I wish to have a tray brought to my room. I feel like being alone with my memories tonight."

"I understand. I'll pass the word downstairs. When dinner is served, I shall bring you a tray."

"Thank you so much, Emma. You've been a brick throughout this entire nightmare. My attention needs to turn to Andy now. He adored Win. This is a tremendous loss for him. Tomorrow I must speak to the estate manager and make certain he understands that Andy is going to need help in training for the future tasks he'll assume, as the new Earl of Winthrop." Sadness tinged Josephine's voice. "I so wish he could have continued with an unencumbered childhood for a while longer. Not that I expect him to take over the reins anytime soon. Obviously. Nevertheless, he *will* have to begin learning the intricacies involved in being responsible for such a vast estate."

"Andy is a fine boy. He will survive this tragedy. I assume you'll continue with your plans for him to finish schooling in Winthrop-on-Hart and then go on to Eton?" asked Emma.

"Absolutely," Josephine replied. "He must be well-educated. That was Win's fondest desire and mine too. Emma, did Uncle Roderick stay on as well as the Drews?"

"No, milady. I heard him say he was going to return to his cottage. In fact, he said to tell you to call on him if you needed anything at all."

Emma left the master suite, and Josephine sat down at the small, corner desk to begin making a list of tasks she needed to complete in the near future. Of course, there were acknowledgments to be sent to all who had remembered Win with floral arrangements and donations to his favourite charities. She also meant to write notes to those who had travelled a considerable distance to say farewell to a wonderful friend. She needed to see to Andy's wardrobe for the coming school year and to send a check for his tuition. She also knew there were countless things like signing legal documents, drawing up her own will, and seeing to Win's estate.

As she sat at the desk, all was perfectly still in the massive house. Besides Andy and the staff, she was completely alone. Naturally, that had been the case on many occasions before, but now realising Win would never be returning, it was as if a giant hole gaped where her heart should have been.

Emma brought a tray to Josephine's room and passed on the news that Tom and Elisabeth were dining with Andy. They had all made the decision to retire to their rooms early. Josephine thanked Emma and said she would place the tray outside her door to be retrieved later. She still was unable to shake the fatigue that had sapped all of her strength. She planned on crawling back into bed as soon as she finished eating the light dinner. There had been such a spread after the service for Win that she really wasn't at all hungry. She ate only because she knew she must.

The meal was consumed, a bath run, and Josephine was back beneath the sheets with the lights out when she heard the door to her room open. It was dark in the suite, and she wasn't able to see who had entered the room. It was completely unacceptable for anyone to enter after the lights were turned off. The only thing she could imagine was that it might be her son, who naturally was exempt from any such rule. Still, she sat straight up in bed.

"Who is it, please?"

There was no answer, but the lock clicked on the inside of the door. She reached over and turned on the bedside lamp.

There stood Oliver, to her utter shock and horror. She could scarcely believe her eyes. While she had been a bit miffed at the detective who'd been assigned to watch over Oliver, she truly hadn't been frightened. Now she was. He stood next to her bed with a large knife in his hand. The expression on his face was pure evil.

"God's nightgown!" she shouted. "What are *you* doing in my boudoir?"

"What do you think, *Countess*," he answered. "I'm here to make you pay the price for taking away my opportunity to be the next Earl of Winthrop. You no longer have my brother to protect you. As you can clearly see, I have a rather nice, sharp knife here. If you so much as make a peep, your throat will be split wide open. Don't think I wouldn't do it. Eventually, they'll catch me, and I'll be returned to that beastly prison. The escape will add years to my sentence, as it is. Thus, murder will only rob me of the remainder of my life. I've already lost some of my best years. The most glorious times of bachelorhood have already passed. I'm a dead man, you see."

Josephine swallowed nervously. She knew Oliver's disposition well enough to know that he was deadly serious. Win had told her many times that, in his opinion, Oliver had always been precariously perched mentally. It now appeared that he had gone over the edge.

She knew precisely what Oliver had in mind. Before that very moment, she would have sworn that she would choose to die before ever allowing that beast to lay a hand upon her. Nevertheless, when faced with the reality of such a choice, she was not ready to die. She had Andy, and he could not lose his mother. He had just seen his father interred. If he lost her, he would never recover. The only thing that seemed remotely possible was for her to make an attempt at reasoning with Oliver.

"Oliver, don't be a fool. You're in enough trouble as it is. You may feel that an injustice was carried out against you, but if you're honest with yourself, you know very well that you deserved the punishment given. Killing me will only bring an end to your life. I cannot imagine you've lost your will to live. We only just buried Win today. Do you want to be the next to compound the tragedy that has befallen Winthrop Manor? Please, Oliver. Put down that knife and leave this room. Leave this house, and I won't even tell the authorities that you were here. You can get on with your escape. Go to London, board a ship and sail to America where you can begin again."

Oliver laughed. "I have you cornered, Josephine, and your precious husband can no longer protect you. Don't think that by blathering platitudes to me, you'll change my mind. I don't intend to get caught, if I can help it. I'll perform the act I've come here for, and then I'll disappear into the night. You *will not* escape, Josephine."

"Oh my God, Oliver. What have I ever done to cause such hatred of me?" she asked.

"You seduced my brother, married him—in spite of your lowly status in society—and produced an heir. If you hadn't entered Win's life, I don't believe he would have married. He always said he was a confirmed bachelor, but you changed all that

"Oh Oliver, how senseless. Win always told me that he understood where his duties lay. He had every intention of following the path expected of the heir. He indeed would have married, even if it had been someone he didn't love. You would *never* have been the next earl." Josephine's voice was shaking, and tears were about to fall.

Oliver merely laughed. "None of that matters now, anyway. Quit trying to wiggle your way out of the mess you've caused." Oliver approached the bed.

She had lost. She would have to face the unspeakable horror that was coming.

"I haven't had a woman in a very long time. I always *did* fancy you. I hope there is such a thing as an afterlife, because it is my fondest desire that my brother is watching this from wherever he has gone."

Josephine openly sobbed.

"Now, now." His voice was cold, unfeeling. "You may find that you actually enjoy this. Think of it this way. Since Win has died, this could be the last time, at least in the foreseeable future, that you'll have the opportunity to pleasure a man." He removed the rest of his clothing and stood stark naked in front of her.

She was revolted. "You are a disgusting pig, Oliver. Perhaps you fancied me, but I always found you loathsome, and I still do." She spat at him.

He lunged across the bed with a full erection. She nearly gagged. He tore at her nightdress until, in only moments, he'd managed to rip it off.

With the bandage still on her leg, Josephine found it difficult to defend herself.

"Yes," he said. "Just as I knew you would be. Nice, big, round tits, and quite a bush down below." He laughed heartily.

Oh. If he only weren't still holding the knife.

Throwing himself on top of her, he began to maul her. How different from the tender gentleness she'd shared with Win. Oliver held the knife at her throat, as he mounted her. "Now, I expect you to at least *act* as if you are enjoying this, milady," he said. "Lie still. Of course, you aren't a virgin. I like knowing that I'm enjoying my brother's leftovers. I'm familiar with Win's anatomy. He should have paved the way nicely for me." With those words, he entered her.

Excruciating pain ripped through her. She shut her eyes and prayed that this horror would end quickly.

He grunted and rolled off. In that climatic moment, Josephine managed to grab the knife from his hand. There was no hesitation about what she must do. She stabbed him over and over again, in the back, the side, and the groin. Finally, she thrust the blade into his heart.

8

❧❧

Blood was everywhere. Josephine was hysterical. She stood, found her robe lying at the foot of the bed, covered herself with it and then rang for Radcliffe. She did not wish all of the staff to descend upon her rooms. It was Radcliffe whose help she required. She did not simply push the button one time, but over and over, alerting him that something was most certainly amiss. In only a matter of minutes, she heard Radcliffe's voice outside her door.

"Milady? Are you, all right? May I enter?" he enquired.

"Yes, yes, please. Please help me, Radcliffe. I've been assaulted by Oliver! I've killed him."

"Oh, dear God!" Radcliffe stepped into the room. "Milady, you need medical attention. I shall telephone for an ambulance immediately."

Tom and Elisabeth had not yet dozed off, and both came fully awake when Radcliffe explained the dire situation. The loyal butler did not add the fact that Josephine had *murdered* Oliver, which of course, was self-defense. Tom Drew grabbed his physician's bag and hurried toward Josephine's suite. When he entered, it was clear that she was in shock. She was entirely too calm. Oliver's body lay at an angle, across the bed.

Tom examined Josephine carefully but gently. As he was performing that task, Elisabeth entered the room. She placed her hand over her mouth in obvious horror at the scene she was witnessing. She had never been fond of Oliver. He'd always had a vile, cruel nature, and had even enjoyed killing animals on the estate just to watch them suffer. Elisabeth and Win had both held him at bay during all the years they had grown up together, keeping him at a far distance. Now, Elisabeth was much more concerned about what was to become of her sister-in-law. She moved to the other side of the bed, pulled up a chair, and sat beside Josephine, holding her hand.

After Tom completed his examination, and listened as Josephine related the entire tale, he told her that she had not suffered any permanent physical damage, but the memory of the savage assault would remain for a long while.

In spite of what had happened , Josephine was of remarkably clear mind.

"Shall I telephone for the coroner?" Tom asked.

"No, Tom. No one is to ever know what took place here tonight. I want you and Radcliffe to find a good spot in which to bury him. I absolutely do not want him in the family cemetery. Find a spot a good way from the house, preferably in one of the wooded areas on the property. Dig a deep grave, for there are scads of wild animals on the property, and if they could, they'd enjoy digging him up."

"Bother the law," he said. "They will *never* become involved. They are presently searching for him elsewhere. They'll never suspect that he stayed here all along. I do not intend to put a blight on Winthrop Manor."

"Good, thank you," was Josephine's only reply.

Josephine and Elisabeth were up until dawn, scrubbing the room thoroughly with bleach. Josephine didn't remember ever having performed such hard labor, but it felt good to be able to put her energy into a necessary task. At long last, they finished. They surveyed the room, top to bottom. It was spotless. They were certain that even when the housemaid came to perform her daily chores, she would notice nothing untoward. Josephine had lighted fragrant candles that burned throughout those long, wretched hours of the night and camouflaged the distasteful odor of death and bleach. They stripped the bed, burning the sheets in the fireplace. Then it was remade.

At long last, Elisabeth was able to return to her own suite of rooms, and Josephine took a nice, long bath. It relaxed her immensely. All she could think about was what Win would have done had he been there when Oliver entered the room. She knew that her husband would have acted precisely as she had. He would have killed him too.

She had never liked Oliver. He'd sneered at her many times for not being of the aristocracy, but his attempted kidnapping of Andy was her primary reason for the near hatred she'd harboured for him. She found it almost impossible to imagine him having been Win's brother.

She had placed Andy's playpen in the shade of the large, old oak tree while she tried to escape from the memory of a world at war by painting at her easel. She had been perfectly content, knowing Andy was safe and secure not ten yards from her. Yet, that damnable Oliver had managed to remove Andy from his playpen, and escape with him to London, where Oliver had prospective parents eagerly waiting to adopt Andy. Those lovely people had no knowledge whatsoever that Andy was not a homeless orphan but an heir to an earldom. Had Oliver succeeded in his diabolical scheme, she might not have had her beloved son, safely sleeping in his own room directly down the hallway from her own.

Win and his parents had discussed Oliver's peculiarities many times in Josephine's presence. He was so entirely different from the rest of the family. While Lady Beatrice had not been the most loving person, Josephine was also certain that Win's mother wasn't mentally unhinged as Oliver clearly had been.

Josephine was quite relieved that he was, once and for all, out of her life. Scotland Yard would be coming 'round to speak to the family regarding the fact that Oliver was still on the run. She had mentally prepared herself for that confrontation and was not at all fearful of its outcome.

After her bath, she dried herself with a fluffy towel from the heated bath warmer, slipped on a fresh nightdress, and crawled back into the newly made-up bed. She briefly wondered if she shouldn't replace the bed with a new piece of furniture, for it would always carry such ugly memories. But then she remembered that it also carried wonderful memories with Win. The spot where she and Win had lain in each other's arms, night after night, after Win's parents were gone and he had managed to return from the Great War. She would forever be grateful that he had escaped from the wretched prisoner of war camp after nearly two years.

She put her head on the soft, down pillow and cried her heart out. She was not crying for Oliver or for having stabbed him to death. She would do it again in a moment, and only wished she might have managed to wrest that knife away from him before he'd performed those revolting, ghastly acts upon her body. No, she was crying for the loss of the man she would always love more than life itself. She felt drained of all energy and wondered if she could continue without him by her side. Nevertheless, she knew in her heart that she must, because she had no choice.

There was Andy, so like his father. And Winthrop Manor, her husband's beloved, centuries-old home. She now had a charge to raise Andy to become a fine man and to make certain that Winthrop Manor's future was safe for another generation.

When she opened her eyes, sunlight was streaming through the windows. From the angle of the sun, it had to be well past the noon hour. Naturally, Emma and Mrs. Shellady, the housekeeper, wouldn't think it unusual for her to have slept so late. It was the day following her husband's burial. She was exhausted, both mentally and physically.

She stretched her body and realised that she was terribly sore from head to toe. Not only from Oliver's brutal assault, but also the accident that had taken Win's life. Thankfully, she had no bruises that would be obvious after she was dressed. Her upper thighs were black and blue, as were her breasts. She would have to make certain not to let Emma see evidence of Oliver's handiwork.

She arranged her hair so that it covered the small cut on her forehead and dressed quietly in a simple dress of black broadcloth. Her skin was still just as lovely as it had been as a young girl, so there was no need to enhance what nature had bestowed upon her. She pinched her cheeks to give them a bit of colour and proceeded down the staircase to face the family.

The first person she saw was Radcliffe, who was carrying a tray down the hall from what appeared to be Tom and Elisabeth's room. They must have dined *en suite*.

"Good day, Radcliffe. How are you on this lovely day? I peeked out of the window in my room and thought perhaps I might take a short stroll after grabbing a bite to eat." Her voice never wavered. She sounded exactly as she always had, albeit perhaps with an added note of sadness due to the loss of her beloved Win.

Radcliffe played his role equally well. "Lovely to see you, milady." He looked her straight in the eye. "Yes, it truly is a splendid day. Andy is already out riding. Cook has a late breakfast waiting for you. She assumed you'd be famished, as you ate such a small amount yesterday."

"I am, Radcliffe, I am," she answered. "I'll send Mrs. Shellady to tell the cook I've finally left my bed."

"Very good, milady. I'm returning this tray to the kitchen, so I'll tell Mrs. Boyle. You might proceed to the dining room. I don't think it will take long at all for her to dish up the fine meal of kippers, eggs, bacon, and herb-stuffed tomato along with your favourite toast from her homemade bread."

Surprisingly, her mouth watered at the thought of such a meal. She would have surmised that the events of the previous night would have ruined any desire for food. "Thank you, Radcliffe. That sounds marvelous." She began to descend the staircase. Suddenly she stopped. Turning her head, she looked straight into the older man's eyes. "Oh, and Radcliffe, I'm not certain you're told often enough how much you're appreciated here at Winthrop Manor. You perform all your duties with such grace and knowledge of the proper etiquette required. I know you're asked sometimes to do things beyond the scope of your regular duties, and you always do them immensely well and without complaint. I shall be going over the budget with the land agent later this week, and I intend to suggest an increase in wages for you."

"Oh, dear me, milady. There's no need for that. I have few expenses, you know. I've always considered it an honour to work in one of the grandest homes in all of Great Britain. That is compensation enough. I would do anything to help you perform the tasks you have before you. Besides, the entire staff just received salary increases at the end of the Great War."

"I know, Radcliffe. Nevertheless, you are one in a million, and I want you to understand my appreciation. Just leave it to me." She smiled.

He shook his head, and mumbled something she couldn't understand, as he continued toward the back staircase leading to the kitchen.

Next, she spotted Mrs. Shellady, the housekeeper. Needless to say, she knew nothing about the horrific acts that had taken place the previous night. Josephine smiled, giving her a warm greeting. She also thanked the older lady for overseeing the details of the funeral gathering. "You performed a lovely tribute to Win."

"Milady, Lord Winthrop was like a son to me. I was here when he came into the world, but I never dreamed I'd be here to see him leave it. The cycle of life was interrupted when he passed away."

"Yes, it was. He took a part of me with him. I truly believe he was my soulmate. Nevertheless, we have Andy to think about now. His father loved him so and always wanted the very best for him. I intend to see that Win's wishes are carried out to a tee. I must look at the calendar. I want to spend a day with Andy in London, outfitting him for his first semester of the coming school year."

"Yes, milady. What a nice thought. I thank God there is Andy. He is almost a perfect replica of his father. I look forward to watching him grow into an impressive fellow, just as his father did." There was a pause in the conversation, as both ladies remembered Win. Each had their own special memories.

Elisabeth entered the blue dining room as Mrs. Boyle placed a steaming plate of luscious breakfast on the sideboard.

Josephine seated herself at the table and tucked into her meal. She was astonished at the hunger she felt. She cleaned every scrap from the plate before it was removed by a kitchen maid. After she had satiated her hunger, she decided she would, indeed, take a stroll around the grounds. What she really had in mind was finding the spot where Oliver had been buried. She wouldn't totally feel complete relief until she knew the grave wasn't obvious. After all, Scotland Yard would eventually pay a visit to Winthrop Manor. She climbed the stairs and made straight for Elisabeth and Tom's room, knocking gently upon the door.

Elisabeth's voice called, "Who is it?"

"It's me, Josephine. May I come in?"

"Yes, of course." Elisabeth opened the door herself. She was dressed in a pretty, flowered robe, and behind her Tom sat in bed reading a copy of *The London Times*.

He laid it aside and greeted Josephine. "You're looking fine this afternoon."

Elisabeth repeated his compliment. "A good night's sleep seems to have restored you."

"Yes. On the outside anyway." Josephine lowered her voice. "Tom, I came to ask if you could direct me to the spot you and Radcliffe buried Oliver. I'd like to make certain for myself that it's undetectable, especially when Scotland Yard returns to tell us they've been unable to find him."

"Yes," replied Tom. "You should know the location. It will put your mind at rest to see that no one will be able to tell there is a body buried there. We did a good job. That old Radcliffe is a worker. He actually did most of the digging, although of course, I assisted. We went down a good six feet, if not more."

"Does the ground above look like a freshly dug grave?" Josephine asked softly.

"No. I don't think there's a snowball's chance in hell that anyone would even notice it. You'll see. Do you want me to come with you?" he asked.

"No. I'd really prefer to go alone. Just try to give me an approximation of the locale."

Tom went on to tell her as best he could how she could find the spot. "There is a copse of large, old willow trees bending over a stream which runs through the manor's property. Do you know of it?"

"Oh, yes, of course. Win and I used to walk out there on summer evenings. It's quite a distance from the house. So, he's buried near the stream? Isn't that a bit of a risk? What if we were to have bad rains or the creek floods?"

"No, he isn't *that* close to the stream. I'm just giving you a landmark to follow. Continue past the stream to where it curves to the right. Walk to the left for a good hundred yards. The woods are very thick there. Lots of birch, oak, elm, and more willow. You'll see a large oak, where someone long ago built a seat 'round its trunk. Probably for lover's trysts." Tom smiled.

"Yes, yes. I know exactly where it is." Josephine blushed.

"Ah!" Tom laughed aloud. "So, you and Win discovered it. Am I right?"

"Well, partly. Win had known it was there since he was a young boy. It's where we would go when we went for strolls at night."

"Then you'll have no difficulty finding the spot. Oliver lies within five feet of that tree. The ground there is typical forest—lots of limbs, wood chips, and leaves. We covered the grave thickly, and even transplanted some of the seasonal flowers now in bloom—daffodils, wild iris, and white violets. Also, some ferns."

"It sounds as if you did a very thorough job. Thank you so much, Tom. I don't know what I would have done without the two of you. I've no concerns about Radcliffe. I've already spoken to him earlier and one would never know that anything unusual took place last night. Just imagine if it had been made public? That newspaper you're reading would have sky-high headlines announcing that I had murdered my husband's brother. A person would have to know the entire story to understand what truly took place."

"You're right, Josephine," Elisabeth agreed. "The front lawn would be filled with reporters. There is nothing Fleet Street loves more than a scandal in the ranks of the aristocracy."

"I know. That's why I absolutely couldn't allow that to happen. You were both so wonderful to help me as you did. I know I can count on you never to whisper a word about this."

"Frankly, Josephine, I can't think of *anyone* who was fond of Oliver. He was an odd chap. Not right in the head. It wasn't just jealously, either. Actually, it seemed to be pure evil."

Josephine shivered, remembering his hands and mouth. God, she was glad he was gone. "Well, I'm going to take a stroll about the grounds. I'll see you later in the day."

"Right," answered Tom.

Elisabeth walked her to the doorway and kissed Josephine on the cheek. "You still have that nasty gash on your forehead. Do you think something can be done about it?"

"Yes. Tom examined it last night. He said it was shallow, and once healed, there are excellent physicians who specialize in such things. It may not be erased permanently, but it will be much less noticeable. Until then, I'm able to arrange my hair to camouflage it."

"You poor dear. You've been through so much. I do hope this is the end of heartbreak and pain for you."

"I'll always have pain, Elisabeth. I no longer have Win, and instead I have sordid memories of his brother. But, I'll learn to live with both.' With that, she opened the door and stepped into the hallway.

Mrs. Shellady was following the upstairs maid, who was carrying a pile of freshly laundered linens.

"Good morning, Mrs. Shellady. It's such a pretty day; I'm going to stroll about the grounds. It may help to cheer me up," Josephine said.

"That's a fine idea, milady. I do hope you have a lovely outing."

9

⧫

Josephine left the house by the front doors, even though it was her intention to wander to the back of the property. She stopped for a few moments, inhaling the heavenly sweet scent of hyacinth, daffodils, and tulips. She adored springtime at Winthrop Manor. The front lawn, from the house to the road, was a solid mass of colour. It was predominantly yellow, with thousands of daffodil bulbs in bloom, replicating themselves over the years. The hyacinth were six rows deep, creeping along the edge of the gravelled drive. Two rows of tulips in various colours ran next to the hyacinth. People from Winthrop-on-Hart were known to drive to the manor each spring to take photographs of the incredible blooms.

When the present flowers faded, azaleas came into full flower–literally hundreds of bushes planted on each side of the glorious mansion. Then came roses. Every species known to man, and at the same time, wisteria covered the outside of the great house. The landscape gardener who had laid out the original plan had made certain that there was never a season when flowers weren't blooming in profusion. Even during the winter months, thousands of winter pansies lined the walkways amid white and red poinsettias. At present, the gorgeous lawns were a riot of colour.

Josephine would have given anything if her darling Win could have been beside her. Nevertheless, he wasn't. She had to begin to accept that, as hard as it might be. She followed a walkway around to the back of the house and then began her leisurely stroll across the lavish green lawn leading to the back of the property where the wooded area began. She knew exactly where she was going.

She found the journey a bit more difficult, as the woods were clogged with underbrush, moss, and ferns. She needed to remind the gardener to clear the underbrush in this area. Continuing on, she came to the small stream Tom had mentioned. She vividly recalled Win having brought her here on a summer evening, kissing her wildly. That was before they'd eloped to Gretna Green. Whoever would have thought their beautiful love story would end the way it had? She had loved him so.

She followed the stream until it made the turn to the right. From there, she had no difficulty finding the old, knurled tree, with the seat built to encircle its trunk. It must have been a favourite trysting place for eons, because there were literally dozens and dozens of initials carved into it. In the past she had only been there at night and had never seen the display that long-ago lovers had left behind.

Searching, she found those that Win had carved for them. *W loves J*. Not far from Win's carving, she saw that *his own* parents had once visited this spot. *R loves B* was quite clearly inscribed there. Appropriate dates were carved beneath the initials. Would someday Andy and a special girl carve their own initials into this special place?

She sat and let her mind wander to those far off days, when everything seemed possible and no obstacles stood in the way of absolute happiness. When she finally stood, tears were streaming down her face. Only a short distance away, she found what she had been looking for.

No one would ever be able to ascertain that it was indeed a grave. Radcliffe and Tom had done a superb job. It simply appeared to be another spot in the vast forest where some wild flowers bloomed. The ground was perfectly flattened. The only way suspicion might ever be raised was if Scotland Yard were to bring dogs to search the property. That seemed highly unlikely. The detectives appeared to be investing their full attention to the probability that Oliver had truly managed to escape.

David Carlisle had notified the estate manager that one of the family automobiles had come up missing after the gathering of guests who attended the funeral had departed. They had little doubt that the culprit had been Oliver. Only he would have known where the garages were and how to obtain the keys. Plus, there had been tyre marks on the gravelled drive directly from the garage to the main road that ran past the manor. The auto had not yet been located. After Radcliffe and Tom had disposed of Oliver, they'd abandoned the automobile Oliver was thought to have stolen. Radcliffe had followed Tom in the Rolls Royce, and then both returned to Winthrop Manor. Supposedly, the detectives intended to return to speak with her later that afternoon.

Josephine stood for a long while at the place where Oliver lay, remembering his body covered with stab marks that *she* had made. The entire incident seemed far away. Of course, she was well aware that many would label her a murderess. It was true. That's what she was. Nevertheless, she felt absolutely no regret and only wished she might have had the opportunity to grab the knife sooner, before he was able to rape her.

Rape! What a disgusting, foul word. Of course, she'd heard of such things, but not once in her life had she thought she might someday be a victim of that abhorrent act. Win, in his gentleness, had always been so kind with her. How in the world those two men had been born of the same parents would forever remain a mystery. Shaking her head sadly, she turned and walked back toward the manor. On the way, picked an enormous bouquet of daffodils.

When she reached the manor, it was tea time. Even though she had consumed a large breakfast only a couple of hours earlier, she found that she had an appetite again. She wandered into the dining room, where Elisabeth, Tom, Andy and, to her great surprise, Uncle Roderick sat. She had planned to find time to ride over to his cottage that very afternoon. She loved him so, and it pained her to see the signs of old-age approaching. He seemed to have aged overnight when the news of Win's death arrived. He'd loved the Win, as if he were his own son. Josephine scurried around to where he was seated, giving him a huge hug and many kisses.

"Oh, Uncle, I'm delighted to see you. I had so little time to see you following Win's services. I am well aware that you don't particularly care for large, social events, and I want to thank you for putting forth the effort to be there."

He planted a kiss on her cheek and said that he had been there because Win was like a son to him, and because she was, and always would be, the light of his life.

"I had intended to ride over and pay you a visit this afternoon. Oh, Uncle, now that I've lost Win, would you consider moving here to Winthrop Manor?" Josephine implored. "Time goes by so rapidly, and it's important to me that we spend as much together as possible."

He smiled and patted her hand. "Dear girl, I've lived at Rose Cottage for nigh on fifty years. It's where I still have memories of Thelma and even of you and Andrew when you first came to me, bereft at the tragic loss of your parents. I have too much emotion invested in that little abode. I promise we'll spend as much time together as feasible, but I've made my plans and they might as well be carved in stone." He laughed. "My life is happy and content. I see the widow, Lucy, whom I met the night you and Win officially announced your engagement. We've even discussed marriage, but both of us are set in our ways, and can't imagine having to start again learning to live with another wife or husband."

Josephine had to laugh at that. She heartily agreed that such a thought was implausible. Though she was still a young woman, only twenty-nine years, she couldn't imagine ever feeling about another man the way she had about Win. It was inconceivable that she would ever remarry.

They all ate Mrs. Boyle's delicious shepherd's pie and freshly baked bread. The estate manager, Ronald Rae, and the land agent, Donald Jones, were also present at the table. Josephine made it clear that she wished for definite dates to be decided upon for a sit-down with Ronald and a look at the account books. She also wanted Andy to have a long discussion with Ronald. Andy had to begin learning the intricacies necessary to oversee such a large holding.

As they continued chatting throughout tea, Roderick brought up the subject of Oliver. Josephine couldn't help it—her stomach somersaulted.

"Why in the world they allowed that scalawag 'compassionate' time to attend his brother's funeral is beyond me," remarked Roderick.

Heads nodded around the table. "Well, you know, Uncle, he has always been a terribly manipulative man. I imagine he managed to convince the authorities that he would be devastated if forced to remain in a prison cell while his only brother was being laid to rest. The truth is, they never gave a whit about one another. Win told me many times how very disappointed his parents were with Oliver. Win had great difficulty having a civil relationship with him." She took another forkful of the delicious pie.

"Yes, well, he *is* my only remaining brother ,and I suppose I *ought* to feel badly about him disappearing," exclaimed Elisabeth. "Nonetheless, if I'm totally honest, I was never able to feel close to him. All he's ever cared about is money, titles and the like. Win and I were never like that. I think the final straw was when I married Tom and Win married Josephine. Oliver got it into his head a long time ago that someday he would still end up as the next earl. I know he didn't expect Win to survive the Great War, and while it's unimaginable, I believe he hoped Win would never return. That's why he concocted that horrendous scheme to get Andy out of the picture. His disappearance would have paved the way for him to succeed our father."

Everyone nodded their heads. It was truly befuddling to anyone with morals and a conscience.

"Where do you suppose he's managed to escape to?" asked Tom.

"My guess would be London or possibly Liverpool," answered Roderick. "He'll undoubtedly try to make it to another country. If he can board a ship, he could probably get to Australia, Canada, or America. It's unlikely, in that case, he'll ever be found."

"I say good riddance," said Andy.

Josephine looked up, a bit startled. "Darling, I had no idea you disliked Oliver."

"Mother, I've known about his attempted kidnapping of me for a long time. How could I possibly respect or trust such a scoundrel?"

"I wasn't aware you knew much about that time," she answered. "You were so small. I'd hoped you weren't aware of it."

"It's always been spoken about rather freely," he went on. "Daddy sat me down one time and explained everything to me."

Relief washed through Josephine. It seemed odd that Win had never mentioned the conversation to her, but perhaps he felt it was private between him and his son.

When tea was complete, everyone went their separate ways. Roderick returned to his cottage with promises that he would see Josephine soon; Donald Jones and Ronald Rae followed Josephine and Andy to the office, where appointments were marked on the calendar for meetings.

Josephine studied the calendar more closely after the two men departed and spoke with her son about a convenient time for a trip to London to ready him for school. Though still not spectacularly happy at the idea of returning to his studies, he accepted the path his father had followed. It was the same one Andy wished to pursue. When he turned thirteen, he would be off to Eton, but he still had three years before that change.

"How about next week?" Josephine asked him. "I've nothing urgent. We could take the train to London and spend a few days there. Perhaps we'll take in the theatre, as well as outfitting you? Would you like that?"

"Yes, Mummy, that sounds wonderful. Did you receive a letter from the school about the clothes I'm going to need?" Andy asked.

"Yes. I have it on my desk in the master bedroom. I'll make certain you have everything necessary to make a proper entry."

"I expect I will," Andy replied. "I just know that I'm going to worry a lot about you without Father to watch over you."

"Sweetheart, I'm a strong person. I shan't be the slightest fearful of being alone here. Well, *really* Andy. I won't actually be alone. Goodness! You'll be home every night. There's an entire staff of people seeing to my every need. And don't forget Uncle Roderick. He'll be here if I need someone, as will your Uncle Tom and Aunt Elisabeth."

"I just worry that Oliver will return and try to harm you," he replied.

"That would be the most foolish thing he could ever do. Scotland Yard has already informed me that they are going to assign a special guard to the house. We shall be well-protected, so put any thoughts like that right out of your head."

Andy smiled and looked relieved. "Oh, that *is* jolly good news. I feel better knowing that. I *am* getting excited about going to school. It's rather lonely here for a boy my age. It will be nice to meet new chums."

"Of course, I know. When I first moved to Hampshire from London, I felt like a fish out of water. So did my brother, Andrew. But, we had each other, which helped a lot. So, I'm thrilled to see you return to classes." She smiled.

"You're smashing, Mummy. I'm so sorry you lost Daddy. Nevertheless, I *do* believe you'll be fine." He came 'round the desk and gave her a big hug and kiss. "I love you, Mum. I hope I can find someone as special as you are someday. That's another thing Father told me."

"What did he tell you about finding someone special?" she asked

"That I was never to pay attention to foolish things like titles and heritage. They aren't important. He told me to wait until I fall madly in love with someone. I asked him how I'd know if I was in love, and he just said I would. I intend to follow his advice."

Josephine tried not to burst into tears. She held her son close to her heart and told him he couldn't go wrong if he only mirrored his father's behaviour.

She had been correct to predict that Scotland Yard would never think to search the Winthrop Manor property looking for Oliver. They stopped at the house later that morning and assured her once again that they felt certain he'd made his way to an English port, where he undoubtedly had boarded a ship. He was probably far away from the British Isles, en route to Australia, America, or Canada. The detectives said that the auto had been discovered, and they were certain that Oliver had taken a train to his final destination.

10

❦

The following Friday, David delivered Josephine and Andy to London in their quest to complete the shopping necessary for Andy to be outfitted appropriately for his first year of attendance at the Winfield Academy. It was not a difficult chore. Harrods had a complete department dedicated to uniforms expected to be worn at English public schools. All the necessary items were grouped in one area of the massive store, and in no time Andy had been completely outfitted in the jackets, trousers, shorts, shirts, ties, and coats required. Naturally, tailoring was necessary, and they made arrangements to have the clothing sent to Winthrop Manor.

It was a relief to Josephine to have that chore accomplished. It was still only June, and Andy would not be starting classes until late August, but it was one more thing she could check off her list. Andy was ten years old, but it was awfully hard for her to accept that. He was tall for his age and already showed signs of a vivid likeness to his father. Perhaps because he had spent the majority of his life around adults, he had a much larger vocabulary than she might have expected from a child his age.

While in London, she also visited an estate agent's office, where she listed the townhouse on Curzon Street for sale. This was not a sad task for her. The memories of that last night were dreadful, and she had no desire to ever set foot in the home again. The agent she dealt with felt the house would sell rather quickly as the location was desirable and the house was in tip-top condition. She intended to sell it fully furnished. There were a few antiques she wished to move to the country, but most of the items were of little sentimental value–especially the beastly bed.

Andy knew none of the details about what had taken place the night of his father's death. Josephine had no intention of ever letting him know the dreadful scene that had erupted, nor Oliver's ensuing assault of his mother, followed by the surreptitious burial. She prayed he would never have to face the truth about such a ghastly affaire. She trusted Tom, Elisabeth, and Radcliffe with every fiber of her being and could foresee no reason that her precious son should ever learn the truth.

After two days visiting the capital, she and Andy returned to Winthrop Manor. The mood in the house was still solemn. The staff had lost the member of the family they'd loved more than any other. They missed his laughter and the jesting that always accompanied his presence. They held great compassion for Josephine. She was still a young, beautiful lady, and most everyone knew she had looked forward to filling that wonderful, old house with a new generation of children who would carry on the stately family name. Obviously, that was never to be.

Josephine settled into a routine. She met with Mrs. Shellady each Monday morning to plan the meal menu and also with the estate agent to go over expenses and discuss foreseeable needs. Everything looked to be in an excellent state of affairs. She was particularly appreciative that she did not have to worry about the god-awful debts Win had run up with his gambling obsession. The estate would show a healthy profit, in spite of the general downturn in economic conditions in England. That was one worry she didn't have to face. She was terribly grateful to Uncle Roderick for having taught her the value of a pound as well as the skills necessary to read a profit and loss statement.

Not long after her trip to London, she received a call from the real estate agent with whom she had listed the townhouse on Curzon Street. She'd received a quite nice offer on the property, and Josephine quickly accepted it. One more task was checked off her list.

As the summer of 1925 wore on and September arrived, Josephine was well aware that there had been no monthly menses since Win's death. She had not been overly concerned, attributing the lack of her monthly to the mental shock associated with the loss of her husband and the ghastly rape.

However, she began to worry. She made the decision to visit a gynecologist in London. Instead of asking David to drive her, she chose to take the train, for she certainly had no wish for him to know her final destination. She used the excuse that she had to meet with the real estate agents about the townhouse on Curzon Street. Some members of the family couldn't understand why she preferred the railway over the comfort of being chauffeured in a Rolls Royce, but she simply stated that it was a nuisance for David to have to make the journey. She said that she rather enjoyed the train.

After leaving the physician's office on that crisp, autumn day, she was in complete shock. The doctor had told her that he was certain she was, indeed, expecting a child. It could not have been Win's baby. She was absolutely positive. They had not had relations since long before the date necessary for a child to have been conceived. That left only one possibility. That gruesome, disgusting pig, Oliver, had planted his seed inside of her. According to the physician, she was a little over four months gone and should expect a delivery date of February the tenth, 1926.

After she'd absorbed the shock, Josephine remembered mornings she'd felt nauseated and even lightheaded and faint. Nevertheless, at the time, she'd never thought to attribute such signs to pregnancy. There'd been so much upset in her life. Surely that had been the reason for physical distress. But she now knew that the physical expression of pregnancy was the cause. She knew what she would have to do. She would lie and say the child had been conceived before Win's death. Dear God, how she wished that were the truth.

She never considered, for even a moment, the possibility of ending the pregnancy. She also could not imagine the remote possibility of feeling love for the baby she carried. Besides, an abortion was a terribly dangerous procedure. She was well aware that women routinely died from botched operations. She would never have done anything to cause Andy to lose the only parent he had left. Besides, it was not the baby's fault that it had been conceived in such an evil manner.

She desperately needed to talk with someone. Elisabeth was the first person who came to mind. Josephine needed a female who would understand the emotions surging through her. Even Uncle Roderick would not be a great help at such an alarming time.

When her train arrived at Winthrop-on-Hart, David collected her at the station. Her mind was still in turmoil when the auto drove through the gates of the estate. However, Josephine was delighted when she saw that both Elisabeth and Tom were on the terrace in front of the house. Instead of continuing to the garages with David, she requested that he pull up directly in front of the entryway. Wasting no time on preliminaries, she walked to the couple, and blurted out the astonishing news that she was carrying Oliver's child.

Elisabeth's first reaction to Josephine's announcement was horror. How could such a thing have happened to the beautiful woman her brother had loved with all of his heart? "Oh, my dear Josephine. Are you absolutely certain? What can I do to help?"

"Yes, I'm certain. I saw an excellent physician in London today. I don't believe there's anything you or anyone else can do, Elisabeth. I only need a friend. I've already given this a great deal of thought. I'll tell people that Win and I conceived the baby before his tragic death." She turned in Tom's direction. "Tom, I assume you'll act as my doctor. I'll need someone close to Winthrop Manor."

"Of course, Josephine," he replied. "You must be about four months along. We'll need to arrange an appointment at my office." He sounded professional, and she appreciated the fact that he wasn't acting emotional.

"Oh, how *can* you have this baby?" cried Elisabeth. "Josephine, how *can* you, *really*? I can't imagine carrying and delivering the child of a rapist."

"I must, Elisabeth. There is no other answer. It isn't the baby's fault."

"I know. Still, under the circumstances, I'm sure Tom would be willing to help you, er..." Elisabeth turned toward her husband.

Tom nodded in the affirmative. "You needn't go through such a wretched experience."

"I know you would help, Tom. Nevertheless, I could never live with myself. It's difficult enough knowing that Win would never have been in the middle of that street if he hadn't been following me, upset and begging me to allow him to explain everything. You see, I feel responsible for one death already. Besides Win, I also murdered his brother. I can't say I'm sorry. He deserved it. However, that action still makes me a murderer twice over."

"This nonsense *must* stop, Josephine. Ridiculous misunderstandings happen in life. You're no more responsible for Win's death than you are for this pregnancy. As for Oliver, that was totally self-defense. No court in the land would have found you guilty. I truly don't know how you can carry a child and go through the anguish of bringing it into the world, knowing how it was conceived. I think you should take a few days to ponder this further. You have to be in shock."

"Will you stand by me, if I decide to go through with the pregnancy?" Josephine asked.

"Of course, I shall. Only *you* can make such a decision. If you're going to go through with it, I admire your courage. Perhaps you're right. I don't know what I would do. Do you honestly think you can love the baby, knowing who fathered it?"

"Yes, I believe I can. When I was first given the news, I thought loving the child would be an impossibility. However, the more I turned it over in my mind, I began to think that I'll feel sympathy towards the baby. What a terrible way for an infant to begin life. Of course, I'll never want him or her to know about the assault and rape."

"No, no. Of course not."

"All right. I knew I needed to tell you at once. Yes, I probably *am* in shock. I'll be all right, though. I feel better knowing I've told you." She turned again toward Tom. "Can I come over to your office tomorrow?"

"Of course," he murmured. "Call in the morning. I don't know my schedule, but I'll definitely fit you in."

Josephine opened the front doors and entered the house. She was terribly distraught, but the staff assumed all the recent events had brought on a sad mood. She told Radcliffe and Mrs. Shellady that she was tired and needed to take a lie-down.

Throwing herself upon the bed, she lay on her back with her hand on her abdomen. Yes, it was swollen and enlarged. Not a lot, but enough so that she could ascertain a difference. Suddenly, she came to the realization that she'd been living in complete denial.

My God, how could I have been so foolish? Soon she began to weep. She'd longed for another child with Win. Now, instead of happiness and joy at the thought of another infant in the nursery at Winthrop Manor, all she could do was remember the horrific attack she'd endured at the hands of Oliver.

What if the baby resembled that ghastly man? Oh, heaven above. She had always thought that Oliver's face resembled that of a horse—protruding teeth, a long face, and a receding hairline, although he was not nearly old enough to be bald. His hair was sandy-red, and he was quite short with a stocky build. The look was not appealing on a man, but what if she had a girl? Win and Oliver were brothers. They were products of the same parents. All she could do was pray that the child would look more like her husband than Oliver. Win had been such a dear, genuinely kind man. He could never have performed the degrading act Oliver had perpetrated. What if the baby inherited Oliver's cruelty?

She sighed, proceeded to undress, and slipped on a nightdress. Then she crawled into her bed. She'd have a tray brought to her room for dinner, since she felt a need to be alone. She yearned for uninterrupted time to think. The most important decision had already been made, but there were still many, many aspects of the unholy mess that she needed to sort through. She tossed and turned all night.

Finally, when morning came, she'd reached the conclusion that the news should, without delay, be shared with the household. She knew she'd passed the point where miscarriages were most prevalent. She would definitely be showing soon. Naturally, everyone at Winthrop Manor would be excited because they would believe Win had left her with a part of himself. Somehow, she would have to act as thought that were true. It was not going to be easy.

Very few people in the mansion knew about the rape, so there was little to no possibility that anyone would guess that the baby was Oliver's. She was glad she'd told Elisabeth and Tom. It was far better that they both knew the truth. Radcliffe, of course, would also figure it out. That didn't cause Josephine undo concern. If anyone in the entire world could be trusted, it was Radcliffe. Sometimes he seemed like a father to her.

Then, there was Uncle Roderick. She would have to be honest, but she trusted *him* with her life. He would be kind and understanding. As for the rest of the staff at the manor, they would have to believe the child was Win's.

The person she considered most was her son. Andy was not the sort to be jealous. In fact, she expected him to be overjoyed. He had been so concerned about leaving her to begin his new adventure at day-school. When he found out she was going to have a baby, he would undoubtedly rejoice. A part of her felt it was unfair to allow him to believe the baby would be his full brother or sister when it wasn't true. On the other hand, it would break his heart to know his beloved mother had been attacked by the uncle he had always loathed. As the new "man of the house" he had been unable to protect her, which would cause him great distress. No, she would never allow him know the truth.

Finally, she rose, ran a bath, and dressed. Normally she would have rung the bell for Emma, but she wasn't ready to make the announcement to her lady's maid yet. She'd be ready to share the news with her Emma by evening when she made preparations for bed, for it was her intention to make the announcement the next evening. It was all rather silly, since Tom and Elisabeth already knew the truth, but it seemed necessary to act out the charade, just as she would have had it been a surprise to everyone. She needed to tell Andy too. She was making decisions in a fog and was well aware of not yet absorbing the full impact of what lay ahead. She was thankful that a baby required nine months to develop, which meant she still had five months to mentally prepare for its arrival.

An hour later, she descended the staircase and entered the dining room. Tom and Elisabeth stood at her arrival. A footman pulled the chair out for her, and Mrs. Shellady brought a plate filled with her favourite breakfast dishes. After Josephine was seated, they all tucked into their food.

"Did you rest well?" asked Tom.

"Yes, thank you, Tom. I did. I'm rather surprised. I suppose I've been going at full speed, what with getting Andy ready for school, and adjusting to my new status in life," she replied.

Both looked at her with concern. Josephine glanced back at them and smiled sweetly. "It's good to see you," she murmured. "I had a rather difficult time falling asleep, but when I finally did, I slept like a baby."

The word baby reverberated off the walls. She noticed Elisabeth react to the word with a sudden nervous tic. Josephine tried to ignore it. Footmen stood behind each chair ,and it was imperative for her to act normal.

When breakfast was over, everyone went their separate ways. Tom had patients to see, and Elisabeth announced her intent to drive over to Cloverdale to pick up the post. Josephine quietly asked if she might ride along with Elisabeth. Josephine planned to have Tom examine her.

Elisabeth knew exactly why Josephine wished to accompany her and quickly answered in the affirmative. Tom left in his own auto and the two women followed shortly thereafter. They spoke as they drove along the empty, country road.

"How do you *really* feel this morning?" Elisabeth asked.

"Honestly, quite well. You can't know what a relief it is to know I can speak with you and Tom about this. I didn't really sleep all that well, but I did a lot of thinking throughout the night. The more I thought, the more I became a bit aflutter at the idea of having a baby. You know I always have adored children. I wanted to have more with Win. Obviously, knowing the baby is Oliver's blunts my enthusiasm, to put it mildly. Still, I've decided to try to feel as positive as possible. Everyone is going to think this child is Win's. I need to force myself to think that way too."

"Josephine, that will not be easy," Elisabeth said.

"Of course, I know that. But, please, help me try. Let's pledge not to refer to the baby as Oliver's. You don't need to pretend it's Win's when we're alone, but I'd appreciate it if nothing is said to dampen my spirits or to remind me of that atrocious man."

"I'll do my best, Josephine. When do you plan on letting everyone in the house know?"

"Tonight," she said.

"So soon? I thought you might wait a bit."

"No. I probably *would* wait if four months hadn't already passed. I don't think it would be wise to postpone telling people any longer. I'll be showing soon, and the staff will guess. So will my uncle. It's also important that Andy be told."

"Yes. I see what you mean. It *will* be fun to have a newborn in the house." Elisabeth smiled. "I hope Tom and I can announce that we're going to be parents someday soon too."

"I didn't know you wanted a baby yet." Josephine was somewhat surprised.

"Yes. We've spoken about it. We aren't desperately trying, but we aren't *not* trying, if you know what I mean."

"Yes, of course. I hope you become pregnant soon. It would be lovely if our children could be close to one another in age."

"Um hum," Elisabeth murmured. "Little cousins to play together. I'd like that."

"Me too."

On the return trip to Winthrop Manor, there wasn't much conversation. She'd seen Tom at his office, and he'd confirmed what she already knew. He said her overall health was excellent, and he expected the pregnancy to go well. It was rather comforting to know Tom would be living in the same home with her for the duration.

As the car pulled into the gravelled driveway, Josephine asked Elisabeth to stop to allow her to step out. She announced her intention to walk to the chapel for a visit to Win's resting place. "I think I'll stop and pick a bouquet of flowers for tonight's dining table. The autumn flowers are in full bloom. I think the house needs some cheering up."

It was another spectacular autumn day. The sun shone brightly and bathed everything in a warm glow, reminiscent of the long-ago May morning in 1914 when Win had ridden past Uncle Roderick's cottage on his favourite stallion, Black Orchid. That had been springtime, and now it was the end of lovely, summer days. Funny. 1914 marked the beginning of so many major changes in her life – the Great War, falling in love with Win, their marriage, and her first pregnancy. It was difficult to believe things could change so dramatically in what seemed the blink of an eye. Eleven years had passed since the beautiful morning when Win had dismounted Black Orchid and a new chapter in her life began.

Following the flagstone path that led to the ancient chapel, she reached the family cemetery in short order. She walked straight to Win's tomb. The inscription had been etched upon the marble sepulcher. She silently absorbed the simple words etched there. JAMES 'WIN' BRADLEY, EARL OF WINTHROP. BORN, 1890 – DIED 1925. DEARLY BELOVED HUSBAND, FATHER, AND SON.

Such uncomplicated words to describe such an extraordinary man. Josephine sat on the marble bench next to the mausoleum. "Win. My darling, darling Win. I'm so sorry I doubted you. It all seems so foolish now. I should have known you would never have betrayed your vows. I'll pray for the rest of my life that you've forgiven me. Oh, my dearest, I'm going to have a baby, and I'd give anything if it were yours. You know everything that happened, don't you? That's what the vicar told me on the day of the funeral. He said you're always with me. I need you, Win. Please be close to me during the coming months."

She laid a single chrysanthemum at the bottom of the tomb. Then turning, she walked slowly back along the path home.

11

❧❧

On her way back to the house, Josephine stopped and picked a large bouquet of flowers from the garden in front of the steps leading to the main entrance—asters, carnations, chrysanthemums, and calla lilies. She took them to the kitchen and asked for a vase. Mrs. Boyle produced a lovely cut-crystal piece that fit the flowers perfectly. "Leave them to me dear. I'll arrange them and see that they're placed on the dining table."

"Thank you so much," Josephine answered. "It seems we've had enough sadness 'round here. I thought perhaps some flowers would cheer things up."

"Absolutely."

Josephine turned, walking back up the stairway, and made the decision to do something she'd never done during the entire time she'd been in residence at Winthrop Manor. She would rummage through the attic and see what old items might be stored from long ago when the nursery had been in use at the manor. It was a bit of an effort to pull the ladder down, and it also seemed to have been some time since anyone had done so. Finally, she succeeded.

She climbed carefully up to the enormous space under the roofline. Cobwebs had to be brushed away and spiders could be seen scurrying about. The entire place needed a good scrubbing. Trunks, boxes, and old pieces of furniture were scattered everywhere. It was hard to know where to begin. She decided to establish a plan. Starting to her right, she worked across the entire area to the wall, and then repeated the same procedure over and over. She made a mental note to remind Andy that if the time ever came when he wished to have his own flat, he should look in the attic for possible furnishings. There were some lovely items.

She came upon a baby cot in the fourth row. It must have been Win's, Oliver's or Elisabeth's when they were infants—possibly all three. She adored it. It was constructed of wrought iron and had elongated poles on all four locales where a canopy could be attached. She had a picture in her mind of the sort of fabric she'd like to choose to have a canopy made. She had already decided that she wanted an all-white room. Later, she would add bits and pieces to add some colour. She noticed various boxes and trunks marked with their contents or the rooms they had come from. This made the task much easier.

After a good deal of searching, she found a trunk labeled NURSERY. Opening it, she found it jam-packed with adorable, hand-knit baby sweaters and myriad other pieces of infant's clothing, adorable stuffed toys, and embroidered small pillows. Evidently these had been used for all three of the children. Lovely cashmere baby blankets also lay carefully packed away. She found a box that read WIN'S BAPTISMAL GOWN. Between two pieces of tissue paper, she discovered an indescribable christening gown. What a treasure. Smiling, she carefully lifted the container from the trunk and set it aside, along with some articles of clothing. In a soft cloth bag, she found a sterling silver cup, baby spoon, and rattle. Another contained a larger set of sterling flatware for a child of perhaps six or seven. She was delighted to have made such a discovery. For the first time, her heart stirred with true happiness at the prospect of having a baby to care for again.

She made several more trips down the ladder, careful not to drop anything or to stumble and fall. She would have to ask Radcliffe to select a good, strong worker on the property to carry the baby cot to the bedroom level and place it in the room adjoining her own. Surely it had at one time served as a nursery. A door led from it to another bedroom, which certainly must have been the nanny's quarters. She realised she had only five months left to prepare for the child's arrival, and much had to be accomplished. Josephine was pleased that she'd made up her mind to announce her pregnancy this evening. In her heart, she was beginning to think of the baby's father as Win. If she allowed her mind to face the reality that it was Oliver's offspring, her joy dissipated. The next five months would be the longest of her life.

Once she returned with the treasures from the attic, she carried them to her chambers. There, she placed them on a top shelf in the room she planned to convert to a nursery. Thank goodness Emma wasn't there. Suddenly, she remembered that she needed to ring Uncle Roderick, inviting him to dine with them at the manor that night. There could be no announcement of the pending birth without him present. She walked to the hall telephone and gave the operator his number.

"Rose Cottage, here," he said.

She smiled. It was so like Uncle Roderick to identify his pretty, rural home when answering the telephone. It had not always been known as Rose Cottage. In fact, his abode had no identifying name whatsoever when Josephine and her brother, Andrew, had arrived there to live with their uncle after their parents had perished on the *Titanic*.

Josephine was the one who'd planted climbing roses on the outer walls of the cottage, as well as over the white-fenced enclosure and the archway above the front gate. In the years since that time, they had grown substantially, and neighbors from miles 'round began referring to it as Rose Cottage.

"Uncle Roderick," she began, "it's Josephine."

"Why, hello, my sweet. How are you? I've rather missed you since returning to my own home. I hope I didn't leave too quickly."

"No, Uncle, not at all. You needed to take care of your livestock and the like, and I needed to get on with my own life. I took Andy to visit Winfield Academy. I think he's going to be happy there. Still, it's good to hear your voice."

"It will take a significant amount of time for you to learn to live without Win. My heart aches for you. I wish there was something I could do to cheer you up, but I'm afraid only time is the remedy for such a tragedy."

"I'm getting on," she replied. "Nevertheless, there *is* something you can do to make me happy."

"Just say the word," he answered.

"I'm sorry to call on such short notice, but I wonder if you might be able to join Elisabeth, Tom, and me for dinner tonight?"

"Yes, certainly. I would enjoy doing so. Is there a special reason?"

"Yes, but I'm not letting the cat out of the bag until you're here." A hint of joy colored her voice.

"Whatever the reason," Uncle Roderick said, "it seems to be making you gleeful. So, something good must have happened, and I'm grateful if that's the case."

"Yes, Uncle. I *am* feeling happy. I never thought I'd be uttering those words so soon after such debilitating grief, but there you have it. Life can be odd. Anyway, I'm so glad you can come for dinner. Would you like to stay at Winthrop Manor for the night and drive back in the morning? Or I could send David to collect you and deliver you back to the cottage, so you needn't drive at night."

"You know, Josephine, I think your latter suggestion is a thoughtful one. I don't like admitting it, but my eyesight isn't as sharp as it once was, and the roadways are awfully dark between here and Winthrop Manor."

"I'm glad I thought to make the offer. Will it be all right if I send David 'round a bit after five o'clock?"

"Yes, perfect, my dear. This isn't a formal affair, is it?" His voice carried a note of concern.

"No, no. Not at all. You needn't wear your dancing shoes," she jested.

"I'm afraid those days are past. I haven't worn my formal attire since that night you, Andrew, and I dined at Winthrop Manor, before you married Win. My God, that was a long time ago, wasn't it? I don't even know if the blasted dinner jacket fits anymore."

"Uncle, you haven't changed one iota since that night." Wistfulness seeped in.

"Oh, my dear. Possibly I shouldn't have mentioned that evening. Perhaps it's too soon to be bringing up such memories."

"It's perfectly fine. I like to speak of past memories. That was the night Win told his parents we were engaged. Lord, they were fit to be tied!"

"Yes, I *do* recall," Roderick laughed. "Nonetheless, it all worked out in the end. Nothing could have marred your happiness that night. I can still see how radiant you looked and the pure adoration on Win's face."

"Yes. Those are precious recollections," she answered. "I'll never forget that night either."

"So." He cleared his throat. "I'll look for David at five o'clock."

"Yes, Uncle. We'll be expecting you. I'm so glad you can make it. I'll see you then." With that, the conversation ended. She placed the telephone receiver back into its cradle and remained seated at the Queen Anne desk in the hallway.

Her mind drifted back to the night Uncle had referenced. She'd been so awfully nervous. It was the first time she'd ever been in a house like Winthrop Manor. Meeting Win's parents had been absolute agony, and his mother, in particular, hadn't made things easier. She also remembered Oliver. He'd been arrogant and rude, making snide remarks about her lack of a title. Placing her hand on her abdomen, she couldn't help but smile. Oliver now lay in the ground on the manor property, dead from her retaliation for his assault and rape. He would never again sneer about lack of a title. Whether she carried a boy or a girl, the child would be styled as a lord or a lady, and she had already been a countess for many years.

When Uncle Roderick arrived at the manor, precisely on the dot of six o'clock, Josephine took him into the drawing room and offered him a drink. He was pleased to accept a gin and tonic, which arrived in short order via Radcliffe. She and Uncle settled themselves comfortably. She decided not to prolong her announcement. She'd taken a lie-down for a couple of hours before her uncle was due to arrive. Then she'd dressed, and Emma had styled her hair in a side-parted bob. She wore a black, tea-length dress with long sleeves and a high neckline. She was, of course, still in mourning.

She had less than an hour to explain the situation to her uncle since dinner would be served at seven o'clock. With a sweet smile on her face, she began to speak, looking straight into his eyes.

"Uncle, I have some news," she said.

"I hope it's not something unpleasant," Roderick replied. "We've had enough of that lately."

"Well," Josephine replied. "Perhaps it's a bit bitter *and* a bit joyous." A puzzled expression crossed the elderly man's countenance. "You see, Uncle, I'm expecting a baby."

He looked exceedingly confused. "How can that possibly be?"

"Uncle, something dreadful happened to me nearly four months ago. I had no intention of ever telling you about it, since I had no wish to cause you unnecessary heartache. Now, however, with this pregnancy, I have to tell you the entire truth. I might have chosen to let you believe the baby I'm carrying is Win's, but I simply couldn't lie to you of all people."

"Go on, Josephine. Whatever it is, I want to know," he said softly.

She proceeded to tell him everything that had happened. It was an ugly tale, and Roderick winced several times while listening to the gruesome details.

"And now, you find yourself expecting a child by that despicable man," Roderick stated.

"Yes, Uncle, that's true," Josephine responded. "However, very few people are ever going to know that. I intend to let the staff, and anyone else who knew Win, think the child is his."

"Doesn't it concern you that Oliver is buried on the manor property?"

"No. The authorities believe he escaped the manor. They've informed me of their belief that Oliver probably made it to London and signed on as a passenger or crew member to either America or Australia. In any event, they have no idea he's dead."

"I fear for you, my sweet girl. What an abysmal story."

"I feel better with you knowing the truth, Uncle. It helps to be honest with you. I could never have kept the truth from the person I love best in the entire world, besides Andy."

"Ah, yes. Andrew. I assume you won't tell him the truth," Roderick said.

"No. I couldn't. It would destroy him to think I'd endured such an awful attack. Also, if he thought the baby was a result of rape, I don't know what he'd do. Really, I don't. Andy is a wonderful boy. He inherited Win's disposition. Thus, he has a strong need to protect me. He's still a child. I think it's far better to let him believe this baby is Win's."

"I agree," Roderick replied.

"So," Josephine sighed. "Tom, Elisabeth, Radcliffe, and you are the only people who will ever know the truth. Radcliffe literally thinks of me as his own daughter, just as you do. I have complete faith that my secret is safe with him."

"Yes, I would agree. Josephine, it will always be safe with me, as I'm certain you already know. I'm so dreadfully sorry you went through such a horrendous experience. Now, you have to go through a pregnancy. If you need to talk, sweetheart, I'm always available to listen. I hope you know that."

"Of course, I do, Uncle. Thank you. I'll be all right. I've already begun to convince myself that this child is Win's. I'll come through everything intact." Josephine smiled.

At that moment, Tom and Elisabeth walked into the room. Roderick rose from his chair. He embraced Elisabeth and then shook Tom's hand. "Well, Josephine has let me in on recent events. I'm dumbfounded at what she's been through, but thankful she had the two of you and also Radcliffe."

Tom spoke first. "Yes, Roderick. It's been a nightmare, really. Still, I'm quite amazed at how well Josephine is handling everything. I think she's going to emerge from this muddle in fine shape. Elisabeth and I will be here to watch over her."

"I'm relieved that you know about everything," Elisabeth added. "It's so difficult for me not to be honest. At least your niece can be candid with the most important people in her life."

"Except for my son." A shadow passed over Josephine's heart.

"It's better that way." Elisabeth gave Josephine an embrace.

Andy arrived at precisely that moment. "Oh, Andy. Hello, darling," Josephine said. "Did you have a nice pony ride?"

"Yes, Mummy. I had to change clothes in a hurry. Now, I'm very hungry."

"Well, the gong should be rung at any moment," she answered. "I'm glad you arrived in time."

"It's so nice to have the entire family together," Andy said.

Roderick turned to his great-nephew. "I'm glad you're here, Andy. Your Mum called me this morning. It's so nice to see everyone, although it's not been very long," he continued. "So, tell me all about your days at Winfield Academy."

"I really like it, Uncle. Of course, it's only been a few days, but I've already met some great chaps. I think there are some who will be real chums. Three of them will be going on to Eton too."

"What time do you leave for school?" Roderick asked.

"I have to be there at eight o'clock, so I get up earlier than I'm used to. Nonetheless, I don't mind. David drives me to and from school. I have five classes in writing, reading and math. We also play sports. The teachers all seem nice. I like having boys my age go play with."

"There are no girls, then?" Roderick remarked.

"No, Uncle. That's fine with me. Girls are such a pain in the neck."

Everyone in the room laughed. "Just you wait, Andy. There will come a time when you won't feel that way," Tom teased.

At seven o'clock the bell rang, signaling that dinner was about to be served, and the family made their way into the dining room.

Everyone was seated around the Chippendale dining table. Josephine tried hard not to let the sadness affect her when she glanced at the empty chair where Win always sat. She knew everyone else was feeling the same way. Uncle Roderick led the gathering in saying grace, and then Mrs. Shellady began to serve. Radcliffe poured wine.

Before everyone began to enjoy what looked to be a splendid dinner, Josephine stood. She tapped the edge of her wine glass to call attention to herself. The footmen were rigidly still, Radcliffe stood quietly, and Mrs. Shellady, who had finished serving, did not leave the room.

Josephine smiled. "I have some news which I know will make all of you smile." Of course, the only person at the table who wasn't aware of what she was going to say was Andy. Mrs. Shellady and the footmen would also be surprised.

"I want to announce that I am expecting a baby. I only just found out the happy news yesterday. I would give anything if Win and I could be telling everyone this together. However, apparently that isn't what God planned." Tears moistened her eyes. "Still, it seems that my wonderful husband left me a part of himself, and I'm extremely happy. So, let's all drink a toast to Win and our new child."

"Oh, Mummy, what wonderful news. I'm so happy. It takes away a lot of the sadness," Andy cried out.

"Yes, darling, it does. We have something wonderful to look ahead to." She returned to her seat. "I'm feeling much less sorrowful. Naturally, I shall always miss your father. Nothing will ever replace the joy I had with him. However, the mere idea that I'm carrying his child brings me great joy."

"Yes. It makes me very, very happy," declared Andy. "When will the baby be born?"

"The doctor says in February. So, you can circle that on your calendar."

"I will." Andy grinned. He stood up and placed his arms about his mother. "I love you, Mummy. That's smashing."

"Yes, Andy, it truly is. I love you too. You'll have such a profound influence upon this baby. What with the age difference, I expect the child will simply adore you. I know I felt that way about my older brother."

"I'll do my best to make him or her love me," Andy replied.

"Even if it's a girl?" Tom asked, smiling.

"Yeah. Even if it's a girl. I'll teach her how to play rugby and football," Andy replied.

With that, Josephine gave him a warm cuddle. Mrs. Shellady and the footmen all waited patiently to give her their love and best wishes. Elisabeth, Tom, and Roderick played their roles to perfection. Each acted genuinely surprised and delighted. They spent the remainder of the dinner chatting about the new addition to the Winthrop Manor family tree. Finally, dessert was served, and it was time for the family to bid one another goodnight.

Josephine made her way to her bed. She was exhausted, but her mind was greatly eased by having been able to tell Uncle Roderick the entire story. She had also taken Radcliffe aside and confessed the fact that a child had been the result of the horrendous attack. Josephine had told Emma about the pregnancy while the maid assisted Josephine with her hair before dinner, but she told her the child was Win's. Emma had been delighted, and for the first time since Win's death, Josephine didn't toss and turn. Instead she fell into a deep, dreamless sleep.

The next morning, she awoke refreshed and feeling better than she had in a long while. After bathing, dressing, and eating a hearty breakfast, she took a walk over the manor grounds. She had made the decision to make an attempt at adding an outdoor stroll to her daily regimen. Tom had told her to increase fresh air and moderate exercise. She found that doing so not only helped physically but improved her mental state. She vowed to continue the practice of a morning stroll, at least until there was a change in the weather.

Time passed. Autumn moved into winter with bitterly cold days and occasional snowfalls. Christmas arrived and she spent hours with Andy during his holiday break. It was lovely to be with him all day long. Still, all in all, Josephine felt far better than she had since she'd faced Oliver's madness. There were moments when she'd have liked to confide in her son, but of course, that was inconceivable. He was far too young to understand, and the truth would only make him sad. Just having his presence at Winthrop Manor all day long was enough. They endlessly talked about his new brother or sister.

"I wish I was going to be here when you have the baby." Andy's expression was doleful.

"Summer won't be far behind, and you'll be here then for a full three months," Josephine replied. "That will allow a lot of time for you to become familiar with the new baby, although infants do sleep most of the time at that age. By next summer, he or she will be active, and you'll have lots of fun playing. I *do* intend to hire a new nanny too. Elisabeth has talked with an agency in London. They have a fine reputation for placement of well-trained young ladies for such positions. So, I'll have plenty of help. Your job will be to continue your education, Andy. You know what your Daddy wanted for you. It's what I want too."

"I know. I like school. I've made rather a lot of friends. They're great chaps. Since you told me that there would be a baby, I've felt better about leaving you, even for the day. It was hard for me thinking of you being alone."

"Andy, I'm truly fine. You must live your own life, darling. Once you finish at the Academy and go on to Eton and then Oxford, there will be little time to look backward. I want you to concentrate on your studies."

"I will be Mummy. I'm serious about my studies. Sometimes I feel older than the rest of my chums at school. Why do you think that is?"

"My guess would be because you're an only child and have been surrounded by adults all of your life. Your Daddy treated you with pride and respected your intelligence. However, Andy, don't throw this special time away with worries beyond your years. I want you to have fun at school too. Enjoy your friends. This is a special time for you. It will never come again."

"I know. Now that a new baby is on the way, I feel less worried about you. I know you'll be very busy."

"I knew you'd see it that way. You haven't an envious bone in your body, Andy. Some people were afraid you'd feel jealous towards the baby. However, I was absolutely certain you wouldn't. You've proven me correct."

"Why ever would I be jealous? I think it's terrific. The baby means a part of Daddy is inside of you."

Josephine clapped her hands. "My precious son. You are wise beyond your years. It won't be very long now. Dr. Tom says the middle part of February. I already have everything ready. The nursery will adjoin my room. Do you know which one I mean?"

"Yes, of course," he answered.

"Well, the nanny will be in the next room, on the other side of the nursery. At this moment, Mrs. Shellady is going through the applications we've received. Many are very impressive. Once she and Radcliffe narrow them down to a reasonable number, I'll interview them. It's very important to me that we hire someone who will be loving and kind. However, a firm hand will also be necessary, if required."

"I don't remember my nanny ever having a very firm hand," Andy said, laughing.

"Andy, my love. You have really never required a firm hand. You were a very easy baby and an even easier child. You still are. I do hope I'm that fortunate again. Your grandmother, Lady Beatrice, always said that Daddy was a wonderful child to raise. However, his brother, Uncle Oliver, had a rather mean streak from the beginning."

"Good Lord, Mummy. Let's not think of Oliver. I never liked him at all. I expect this new baby will be just like you or Daddy."

"Yes, me too." She smiled. "So, do enjoy your last few days before classes resume and return to school free from care about me."

"All right, Mummy." Andy leaned forward and kissed her on the cheek. "I rather hope for a sister who will grow up to be as pretty as you."

"Andy, you are every mother's dream." She gave him a kiss in return. "I love you so much."

"And I love you, Mummy. Now, I'm going to ride over to Uncle Roderick's. I haven't seen him since Christmas day. He looked as good as always, and I'm glad he'll be here to comfort you when the baby is born "

"Yes, so am I," she answered. "He's such a dear. Yes, go and spend some time with him. He'll love seeing you."

Josephine was very large and exceedingly uncomfortable. While carrying Andy, she had experienced no discomfort, but this child continually kicked, to the point that it actually brought pain to her abdomen. It was as though the little thing wanted out of the prison of her womb. Josephine looked forward eagerly to the delivery date. She prayed the infant would calm down, once it had been released from its confines.

January passed quietly. Though the weather remained bitterly cold, there was no snow. Josephine spent the majority of the month interviewing applicants for the position of nanny. She was greatly impressed with many of the girls she spoke with, but none met her exact qualifications. She felt she would instantly know when the proper person presented herself.

Finally, as the stack of applications dwindled, a lovely young lady made her way to the door. Mrs. Shellady placed her in the small waiting area off the great hall. The girl's name was Hope Reed. She was a truly lovely young lady with long blonde hair, blue eyes, and a sweet smile. Mrs. Shellady interviewed her first and had been impressed with her credentials. She had completed training at a fine London school for household help of the finest grade. After spending over a half hour with Hope, she passed her along to Josephine.

From the moment the countess set eyes on her, she was almost one hundred percent certain she had found her nanny. They spoke of many topics, and then Josephine asked the one question she had asked a dozen or more times, only to be given a disappointing response. "What is your philosophy regarding discipline?" she put to Miss Reed.

Hope sat silently for a moment, as if she were trying to decide whether to be honest or not. Finally, she spoke. It was obvious that honesty was the only way she knew.

"Countess, I'm not certain I truly have a philosophy regarding discipline. That would be as if I were treating each child as though their make-up was the same as every other child's in the universe. It's my belief that every youngster is different, and I have to take that into account. It's up to me to understand what is creating a particular disciplinary problem. If, for instance, a child is causing havoc in the nursery, I feel it's my responsibility to figure out what need isn't being met within his or her personality. Then, I will try to find a more productive means to meet that need—more productive for the child and for the atmosphere as a whole."

Josephine had been looking for just such an answer for weeks. So many prospective nannies gave a pat answer, such as "placing them in the corner, taking away a privilege, or ordering the child to stand in the hallway for a given period." The young lady in front of Josephine clearly believed in finding the root cause of disruptive behavior and then meeting it with a way that would benefit the child and anyone else present. Josephine was heartily in agreement.

"Miss Reed, I have hoped to hear that sort of answer forever. I like your attitude, and I think you will make a fine nanny. Of course, you are aware that there will only be one child in the nursery at the beginning of your employment. However, my sister-in-law, Elisabeth Drew, announced only last week that she is expecting a baby in July. So, you will have two infants not far apart in age. Your duties in the beginning will be to concentrate upon the baby I'm about to deliver. However, that will change in the summer. I expect you to act in a nursemaid capacity to both my baby and Elisabeth's. I assume you're familiar with that role?" Josephine asked.

"Yes, indeed, Madam. Nappies, rocking, games appropriate to the infant stage, nighttime care—so you aren't awakened during those hours. I assume you have, or will be acquiring, a pram? So, my duties would include outings on warm days. I assure you my eyes would never leave the infant. No harm would ever befall him or her on my watch."

"Excellent," replied Josephine. "I had a terrible experience when my son, Andy, was an infant. He was kidnapped."

"Oh, heavens above! How dreadful. I hope he wasn't in the care of a nanny?"

"No, while I hate to admit it, he was in *my* care. So, I'm very much concerned that whomever I hire will be eagle-eyed and watchful for any foul play."

"You may rely on me, Countess. I'm fully aware of the trust being placed in me. I promise that no harm will come to any child under my watch."

"Well, I'm very impressed Miss Reed. I'd like to offer you the position of nursemaid/nanny. It would be my preference if you can begin quite soon. It's important to me that you familiarize yourself with the house and premises."

"I'm available to begin whenever you wish," the girl answered.

"Well then, let's say a week from today." Josephine smiled. She went on to give the young lady a figure for wages, which brought a smile to Hope's face.

"That's more than generous, Countess. Thank you. I *am* assuming I'll be living in?"

"Yes, of course," replied Josephine. "I'll have Mrs. Shellady show you to your rooms, as well as the nursery and the rest of Winthrop Manor. Feel free to wander about the grounds. We'll look forward to having you join us."

Hope Reed responded in kind with a broad grin. "I'm thrilled to be joining your household and will try my hardest to live up to your expectations."

"I have no doubt that you will." Josephine gave a welcoming, warm smile.

With that, Josephine summoned Mrs. Shellady and instructed her to show Hope the premises, and also to introduce her to the rest of the staff. Josephine was greatly relieved to have this most important task behind her. Hope appeared to be exactly the young lady she had been praying for. Everything was settled and now all Josephine had to do was await the arrival of her new son or daughter.

12

❧❧

On February 21, 1926, at seven in the evening, Josephine's water broke. She was tremendously thankful that this signal, which indicated the beginning of labor, happened in the evening when Tom was present. Having experienced childbirth before, Josephine was much less troubled than she had been with Andy. Andy had been such an easy birth. While there had been several hours of labor, she didn't remember the experience as one that had been excruciating painful.

Unfortunately, the same couldn't be said this time around. Almost from the first labor pain, Josephine was in agony. Tom examined her many times throughout the night, but little progress was being made. Finally, at nearly eight o'clock the following morning, he announced that the baby appeared to be breech. That meant that the infant was presenting legs first—a major complication.

Tom spent the next several hours attempting to turn the infant, so that it might be delivered head first, as was the normal procedure. Finally, he *did* accomplish his goal, but Josephine was nowhere near prepared to deliver. She had scarcely dilated, in spite of the time that had passed. It almost seemed as if her body didn't wish to give up the baby. More hours passed, and by morning of the third day, when Josephine was nearly at the end of all strength, Tom made the decision to deliver the child by Caesarian Section. He wished he had placed her in hospital for such a procedure.

Josephine was past the point of caring how the child was extracted. She was administered ether, in an attempt to lessen the pain.

At long last, Tom plucked a nine-pound, six-ounce baby girl from the mother's womb. It was the largest baby he had ever delivered, and it made clear why a natural birth had been out of the question. It was February 23, 1926.

Immediately upon the delivery, pain medication was administered. The baby appeared to be healthy. She howled and wailed while Hope, acting as nursemaid, took her from Tom and gently cleansed her. The newborn was then placed at Josephine's breast. Josephine had decided to name the child Estelle Janine, if a girl.

Estelle immediately grabbed hold of her mother's breast and began to nurse. Unlike her experience with Andy, Josephine cried out in pain. Tom was surprised, because generally once a baby began to nurse, both mother and child started to form a closeness with one another and peace reigned. However, tears literally streamed down Josephine's face, while Estelle eagerly sought to fill her tummy with milk from her mother's breast.

Finally, Tom picked up the infant and examined her mouth. To his utter amazement, he discovered several upper and lower teeth! He had studied this sort of rare condition, but it was his first experience with it. No wonder Josephine had been in pain. Estelle was literally chomping and gnawing at her mother. Tom could see teeth marks on Josephine's breast.

He handed the baby to Elisabeth, who often acted as his assistant. Then, turning to Hope he said, "Please run to the kitchen and have the cook prepare some formula for this child. She cannot nurse. She will cause harm to Josephine if she continues to do so. The cook will know what to do. This isn't something frequent, but I *did* make certain we had the necessary items to concoct a formula in case it was required. Mrs. Boyle also has formula bottles available. Have her fill one and bring it back here as quickly as possible."

Such bottles and the like had been in existence since the late 1300s in both England and America. Because Estelle had been born with teeth, Tom would teach Josephine how to express her own milk and then the baby could be bottle fed.

Elisabeth glanced at her husband with relief and whispered to him, "I hope this isn't some sort of omen." He simply rolled his eyes heavenward. It had been a most strange beginning to Estelle's life.

Elisabeth and Tom welcomed their own precious daughter, Susan, as expected in July of 1926. Susan embellished Winthrop Manor in the way Andy had when he was born. The entire family and staff adored her. She was a beautiful baby, with blonde hair and blue eyes, resembling Lady Beatrice's side of the family.

On the other hand, Estelle's hair was the sandy-red, which Oliver had sported, but she *did* have Josephine's pretty, green eyes with long lashes, and overall, was also a lovely baby.

In the beginning, Estelle's life at Winthrop Manor was truly joyful. She was a sweet baby and everyone took to her with fondness. Every attempt was made to forget that she was the product of rape. She was also a pretty baby and Josephine felt truly fortunate.

On a rainy day both the elderly, former cook and Winnie were sitting in front of a cosy fire. Both women welcomed Estelle warmly, giving cuddles and kisses. She sat on Winnie's lap while a storybook was read to her. As often happened, Vera dozed off and appeared to fall into a deep sleep. Winnie removed Estelle from her lap, took her by the hand, and led her into the small parlour.

"We're going to play a new game," she announced to the little girl.

"Oh, what is it called, Miss Winnie?" Estelle's voice carried an excited tone.

"It's called 'I'm the daddy and you're the mommy,'" Vera's companion answered.

"What do we do?" Estelle continued. "How come I'm the mummy?"

"Because I'm much bigger than you are, just like your Daddy was before he passed away."

"Oh, all right. I see." The sweet child looked at Winnie with absolute trust in her pretty eyes.

"All right then, let's pretend," said Winnie. "You take off all of your clothing."

"Why, Miss Winnie? Mummy says I should never do that in front of a stranger."

"Estelle, sweetheart. I'm scarcely a stranger. Goodness, who knows you better than I do? Isn't that right?"

"Yes. I guess so." The child looked somewhat confused. Still, in spite of her mixed emotions, she *did* trust Winnie, so she proceeded to pull off her little pleated skirt and the sweater she wore over it. Next came her tiny undershirt, and finally, the knickers. She stood there in front of Winnie stark naked and shivering.

"Now," said Winnie, "you lay down on the sofa over there." She pointed to the couch covered in a pretty chintz fabric composed of birds and lovely flowers on a white background.

Estelle followed Winnie's instructions, but she had an odd feeling inside that she didn't like the game at all.

Winnie proceeded to undress as well. Estelle was truly amazed. Nothing in her tender years had ever prepared her for such behaviour. Her voice dropped to a whimper. "Are you really sure this is all right, Miss Winnie? I've never seen a grown-up with no clothes on."

"That's what makes the game fun, Estelle. It's filled with surprises for you."

"Oh, I see," Estelle mewled again. As soon as those two words left her mouth, Winnie was climbing on top of her. Estelle was very frightened, yet she hadn't the slightest notion of what to say. She lay perfectly rigid as Winnie lay across her little body, and began to slide her hands downward.

"What…What are you doing? I don't think I want to play this game anymore." Estelle cried, tears welling in her eyes.

"Oh, Estelle, you'll like it, I promise" replied Winnie. "You must trust me. If you don't I shall be very hurt. You don't want to hurt me, do you?"

"No. I don't guess so," the youngster whimpered.

By that time, Winnie had inserted a digit into Estelle's private place between her legs. She began to move her finger back and forth, rapidly. Estelle did not like the sensation, and an inner voice told her that something was amiss. She made an attempt to sit up, but Winnie held her down with her other hand. Winnie was strong. Estelle looked up at the older woman's face and she was very frightened when she saw a weird grimace. It was not the face of the lady she had grown to know and love.

Estelle cried out. "Stop!" But there was nobody to hear her little voice.

Next, Winnie moved her head further downward and actually placed her mouth where her finger had been a moment before.

Estelle began to wiggle and push her away. It seemed as if Winnie wasn't even able to hear her. She looked like she was completely unaware that Estelle was simply a little, confused child. Then, suddenly, before Estelle could utter another sound or make another move, Winnie groaned and her entire body shook from head to toe. She lay for a moment on the terrified child, and then got up, acting as though nothing odd had occurred.

"Now, let's get you dressed, sweet girl." Winnie reached out the same hand that only moments before had done evil things to Estelle.

The child quickly stood up, and grabbed for her clothing.

"Here, my dear. Let me help you," Winnie said, as though butter wouldn't melt in her mouth. "For playing that game so perfectly, I'm going to give you a very special gift."

"A gift? What sort of gift?"

"Just about one of the most beautiful gifts a sweet girl like you could want," came the reply.

"What is it?" Estelle had a note of disbelief in her voice.

"A brand new, beautiful dolly," Winnie answered.

"A dolly." Really?"

"Yes. Wait right here. I have it in a box in my closet." She left the room momentarily, once again fully garbed. She quickly returned with a rather large box under her arm and set it down in front of Estelle. "Open it, darling. It's all yours."

Estelle tentatively approached the box and reached for the lid.

"Wait just one moment, dear. I want you to understand that our game is to remain private. It's just between you and me. Grown-ups cannot ever know about it. If they knew, they might not want you to play it knowing you were being giving such delicious gifts for playing with me. Do you promise to keep it a secret?"

Estelle eyed the box. Oh, how she wanted to see that dolly. What had happened wasn't really so terrible – not if she got a dolly for a few minutes of playing. "All right," she said to Winnie. "I promise."

"Oh, I just knew you would. You are always such a well-behaved and sweet girl. Each time we play this game, I'll give you a special gift. There are so many things I know you would love to have. I remember when I was your age. My nanny played this same game with me, and I got dollies and dolly houses and a rocking horse – just so many things."

"Yes, but, won't Mummy wonder where all of these toys are coming from?" the wise child questioned.

"Oh, we'll tell her that gentle Vera asks me to purchase these things for you. Vera doesn't have a very good memory any more. She won't remember if she made such a request. Your mummy loves Vera. She would never deny her the pleasure of spoiling you a bit with presents. Your mummy is very soft-hearted."

Estelle proceeded to open the box. There lay a gorgeous doll dressed in a blue velvet gown with pearls on the bodice. She had long, golden curls and lovely blue eyes. Estelle had never seen such a beautiful dolly. "Oh, oh, Miss Winnie. She is so pretty. I love her. What shall I name her?"

"Whatever your heart desires, my angel," Winnie replied.

"I shall call her Josephine after my mummy, but I'll shorten it to Josie. Do you think that would be fine?"

"Yes, of course. Absolutely fine. And, this time, you can tell your mum that I gave Josie to you just because we're special friends and I've grown so very fond of you."

"All right. I'll do that. Mummy will think she is ever so lovely."

"Just remember, that our game is a very special secret," reiterated Winnie.

Estelle was so overcome with joy at the receipt of such a glorious gift that she would have agreed to any request made of her. "I'll remember, Miss Winnie. Now I think this is a wonderful game."

From that watershed moment, Estelle's life and her behaviour became extremely erratic. She and Winnie played the game often. A lovely gift was always waiting. The child was so young, so unaware of the evil in Winnie's heart. Estelle simply complied with Winnie's wishes and collected her reward. She had no idea that the wicked acts were changing her. Rage was building deep inside, and although she was but a tyke, that confusion and anger would find its way to the surface in wretched acts.

When Estelle turned six, events took a violent turn for the worse. She became unruly and difficult to handle. She demonstrated above-average intelligence, but her vocabulary was completely inappropriate for such a young child. She used terrible words, and Josephine couldn't imagine where Estelle had heard them. Nobody, to Josephine's knowledge, had ever used such language at Winthrop Manor.

She discussed the problem with Hope, who said she had no explanation except that generally when children picked up such vocabulary, it came from having heard adults speak that way. Estelle also talked naughty to Hope, as well as to Josephine and her aunt Elisabeth.

Then they began to notice repeated lies. The lack of truthfulness seemed designed to make trouble for little Susan, Elisabeth's daughter. Josephine discussed the problem with Elisabeth, who in turn approached Tom.

Josephine made an appointment at his office on Estelle's sixth birthday. Estelle had taken to spending quite a good bit of time with Vera, but Winnie Lawrence was always nearby. Even at such a young age, Josephine began to recognise that something about the child was abnormal, except that she exhibited above average intelligence, but of an odd variety.

Josephine made the trip to Cloverdale alone. When she was ushered into Tom's office, she sat down in a chair facing his desk. Before she could open her mouth, tears began to well in her eyes.

"I don't think I need to enquire as to what is causing you such terrible upset," Tom began. "It's Estelle, isn't it?"

"Oh, yes, Tom. Something just isn't right about that child. I *want* to love her, but you've seen her behaviour with your own eyes. I'm at a loss as to what to do. Hope is too. She's received training in Early Childhood Education, as you know. However, she says she's never witnessed anything remotely like Estelle's behaviour. She *used to be* very sweet, but in the past year she has become a holy terror. She uses truly *filthy* words, and her actions aren't those of a small child. Elisabeth and I continually have to make certain she doesn't harm Susan. Tom, she has even tried to make sexual advances toward her little cousin."

"What sort of sexual advances? My God, Josephine. Susan is *my* daughter too. That's very strange for a child of her age and it concerns me. What exactly does Estelle do?" He asked.

"She gets on top of her and makes movements of a sexual nature, um, well, mimicking adults having intercourse." The conversation was excruciatingly difficult for Josephine, even though Tom was her brother-in-law. "I've never seen a six-year-old act in such a manner."

"Nor have I," answered Tom. "I hate to say this Josephine, but I'm beginning to think she has inherited her biological father's evil streak."

"Surely you can't believe that." Josephine was astonished. "Is that sort of thing even possible?"

"There has been very little research done on the subject, so I'm not able to offer a definitive answer. Do you know anything about what Oliver's behaviour was at her age?"

"Not very much," answered Josephine. "I *do* recall Lady Beatrice saying that he had been a very difficult child as compared to Win. Nonetheless, I've heard many mothers make those sorts of comments. Lady Beatrice never spelled out exactly what she meant by 'difficult.'"

"There *is* the possibility that this is simply some sort of phase she's experiencing, and she'll grow out of it," Tom replied.

"My God, I hope so," said Josephine. "If it's a phase, it's not nice of me to say this, but Tom, I don't like her very much. That's simply a beastly, wretched comment for me to make."

"If it makes you feel any better, I don't believe anyone at Winthrop Manor cares for her very much. Hope has told me she makes every effort to show love and affection to Estelle, but the child has even spit in her face. I understand she spends a lot of time with your retired cook—Mrs. Whitaker, isn't it?"

"Yes. She'd been with the family for a very long time, as I believe you know. She enjoys Estelle's company, and Estelle appears to love Vera."

"Do you know anything negative about Mrs. Whitaker's background?" Tom asked.

"No. Remember, I only came to Winthrop Manor at about the time she retired and you diagnosed her with dementia. Why do you ask?"

"I only wondered if Estelle's time with her could be having some sort of negative effect on the child. Have you ever heard *her* use unseemly language or show any unusual traits?"

"No. What sort of traits? You know, of course, she was involved with Oliver in the kidnapping of Andy. However, that was Oliver taking advantage of Vera's mental decline. At least that's what Win believed. I do too."

"That's undoubtedly true. What about the companion who watches over Vera?"

"Winnie? Gosh. She seems to be the sweetest person in the world. I didn't hire her. She was on the premises when I arrived. Apparently, she has excellent references."

"Still, you should keep an eye on Estelle—a close eye," said Tom. "I'm somewhat concerned about my own daughter. From what you've told me, Estelle is already demonstrating unsavory behaviour toward Susan."

"Yes, I know. I think I'm going to have to take over disciplining her. Hope and I agreed when I hired her that children should never be spanked.

However, Estelle seems to be crossing boundaries right and left. She has to be made to understand that her demeanor is unacceptable."

"I'm afraid I have to agree, Josephine. Perhaps the problem lies with the fact that she has no father? Nevertheless, I've known many a child in the same predicament who don't manifest such troublesome behaviour. Look at Andy, for example."

"No. I don't think that's it, Tom. I wish Lady Beatrice were still living. I have a sneaking suspicion I'd learn she's mirroring Oliver's behaviour. God help us all if that's the case."

Tom got up from his chair and walked to Josephine's side. She also rose. He patted her on the shoulder. "Let's not jump to conclusions yet. Perhaps it truly *will* be just a phase," he remarked.

"Maybe, Tom, but there is going to be a definite change in disciplinary action, and please, don't let anyone keep any information about any deplorable behavior from me."

"I promise. You'll be kept informed." He escorted her out the doorway.

Josephine *did* hold firm to her vow to take matters into her own hands when it came to disciplining Estelle. Nearly every day the child did something unacceptable, and Josephine found herself swatting her little bum repeatedly.

Strangely, Estelle never cried, screamed, or promised she would never act badly again. She simply accepted the punishment, glared with a wicked expression at her mother, climbed down from Josephine's lap, and ran to Vera's room. Vera, who had no concept of the difficulties facing the family when it came to Estelle, held her, rocked her, and whispered sweet words.

Winnie also took Estelle's side and never punished the girl for bad acts. Instead, they played their game.

Estelle and Susan were both seven years old, and life at the manor was a nightmare. The adults had put off allowing the two children to spend much time together as long as possible, hoping that with maturity, more appropriate behavior on the older cousin's part would arrive. There *were* times when the two played nicely, but most often Estelle seemed to manipulate Susan into trusting her, only to eventually harm Susan in some way or another.

One day, Hope discovered Susan hanging upside down in the laundry-shoot, gagged and blindfolded! Hope rapidly untied the child, who began to cry hysterically.

"How did this happen, Susan? Who did this?" Hope asked, knowing full well what the answer would be.

"Estelle grabbed me. She said I could play with her dolly," Susan hiccupped. "When I picked up the dolly, she put a scarf 'round my mouth and eyes and dragged me to the dirty clothes place."

Hope was beyond angry. If Susan had not been fastened tightly, she might have fallen straight downward to the first level, where the kitchen and laundry facilities were located. It might very well have ended her life.

While Susan sobbed to Hope about what had occurred, Estelle was in the corner of the nursery, setting the small children's table for a tea party with doll's dishes. She looked at Hope with a look of pure innocence, as though she knew nothing about the incident.

Hope walked over to her, and taking Estelle by the collar on her candy-striped dress nearly shouted. "Estelle! You are a devious child. I've never said anything like that in my life to you or any youngster. However, you are old enough to know better. Seven years is far too old to be placing your little cousin into harm's way. Susan might well have been badly injured or even killed. Why do you do such things?"

"She took my doll away from me, Nanny. Mummy gave me that dolly for Christmas. Susan was going to throw it down the laundry place. So, I taught her what it feels like if she'd done it to the dolly."

Hope was outraged. She knew Estelle was lying. "I'm sorry Estelle, but I don't believe you. I've caught you in several lies before. I haven't any notion as to why you want to behave in such a naughty way. You are the most mischievous and, yes, evil child I have ever had to deal with. You make your mother very sad. Unfortunately, I shall have to report your behaviour to her again."

"Go ahead. I don't care," Estelle said. "I don't even like her."

"What a wicked thing to say about your own mother. You are a nasty child, Estelle," Hope retorted.

"Susan, follow me. I don't want to leave you alone here in the nursery with Estelle." The little girl followed Hope as they left Estelle behind.

As soon as Hope and Susan disappeared, Estelle followed her usual pattern. She ran to Vera's room.

There was consideration given after that event to sending Estelle away to a boarding school. Josephine was terribly reluctant to do so, since the child was still quite young. Few schools even considered accepting a child at that age.

However, only a few weeks later Hope was overseeing the two cousins as they seemingly played quietly together in the nursery. Estelle's overall behaviour appeared to have improved to a slight degree, which was why the two were once again being allowed to interact.

Suddenly, a blood-curdling scream erupted from little Susan.

Hope ran to Susan's aide. It was instantly apparent what had occurred. Estelle had thrown a pair of adult scissors at Susan. Blood was pouring out of the child's right eye. Hope called out for help, and David Carlisle responded. "David, please help," the young nanny cried. "Susan must be taken to hospital at once. Estelle has thrown a pair of scissors at her, and I am terribly afraid that she has permanently injured Susan's eye."

David swept Susan into his arms and carried her to the Rolls Royce. Hope accompanied the child to Winthrop-on-Hart hospital. After immediate medical care was administered, Hope was informed that Susan's eye had been damaged, but in time would recover. Susan would have to wear a bandage over the eye for quite some time. Hope was nearly sick to her stomach. Estelle needed to be harshly disciplined. How on earth would she break such ghastly news to Elisabeth and Josephine?

Back at the manor, Elisabeth was devastated when Hope shared the details with her. Naturally, Elisabeth rushed to Susan's bedside accompanied by Tom. A top eye specialist arrived from London. After examining Susan, he reached the same conclusion that the physician at Winthrop-on-Hart hospital had formed. By the grace of God, the scissors had missed the pupil of the eye and it was expected to completely heal in time.

Josephine had arrived at hospital too, sick at heart for her sister- and brother-in-law and mostly for her sweet niece. Josephine didn't believe for one moment that what had transpired had been an accident. Susan stated clearly, and with no confusion that Estelle had thrown the scissors at her with direct aim at her eye. It had been no game.

After that devastating event, a decision was made that the two cousins would no longer be allowed to spend time together. Josephine was at her wit's end. It seemed the only plausible solution. Estelle had only continued to worsen as she'd grown older.

Tom and Elisabeth moved back to their own home in Cloverdale in a desperate attempt to protect their beloved daughter.

Josephine continued to catch Estelle listening behind doors on the infrequent times when the countess had a friend paying a social call to Winthrop Manor. Even when the vicar came by the child secreted herself behind furniture in the drawing room in order to overhear conversations. She was underhanded and sneaky. At long last, Josephine excused Hope from having to watch over her, and the lovely nanny was given only supervision of Susan in Cloverdale. The two cousins never saw one another.

❧❧

Strangely, Andy, Vera, and Winnie were the only persons in the manor household whom Estelle actually seemed to like. When Andy *was* home from school, Estelle behaved like a different child. She brought him books, asking him to read them to her, and as she matured she took him to her room and showed him the drawings she had done as well as embroidery work she had completed. Andy never saw the side of Estelle the rest of the family had to cope with. It was confusing.

Josephine made attempts to draw him out regarding his thoughts about her, but Andy said he could see nothing amiss. To him, she seemed like a perfectly normal child.

Hope made every attempt to make Andy understand what the family regularly faced, but again, he found it difficult to believe her stories. Instead, he began to side with his sister and reached the conclusion that for some inexplicable reason everyone in the household had it in for Estelle, except Vera and Winnie. There was absolutely no consideration given to attempt a conversation with Vera, since her mental abilities made such a thought absurd. Instead, Andy thought everyone seemed google-eyed over Susan.

13

❧❧

After Andy graduated from Eton in 1937, he returned home for the summer and began to learn the intricacies of operating an enormous holding like Winthrop Manor. He had been taught rudimentary tasks from the time his father had died. He was eighteen and would be starting Oxford in the fall. When he reached his majority at age twenty-one, he would become the Earl of Winthrop.

Andy excitedly returned to Winthrop Manor thrilled to see his mother and Estelle. Tom, Elisabeth, and Susan once again moved over to the manor to be there for the summer months in order to see as much of Andy as possible. Susan's eye had completely healed after repeated surgeries and the youngster had to wear special eye glasses. A close eye was kept on Estelle. She acted the perfect angel for almost the entire summer. However, apparently expecting her to maintain proper decorum for an entire three months was more than anybody should have expected.

On Andy's second-to-the-last day home, he asked Estelle if she would like to accompany him to the chapel connected to the main house.

Estelle readily agreed, although she always refused to take part in any of the religious services in the Anglican Church and maintained that she did not believe in God. Andy appeared to be the only soul on Earth she cared at all about, besides Vera and Winnie, so no matter where he was going, she would undoubtedly have agreed to go with him.

He held her hand as they walked down the stone pathway leading to the chapel.

When she and Andy reached the chapel door, he held it the open for her and she entered. Andy followed. He walked down the center aisle and stepped in front of the main altar, where he knelt to pray. Estelle sat down in a pew next to him. He spent a good deal of time in that position, praying for his family. In particular, he asked God to watch over them during his absence.

Andy was about to rise, when Estelle slipped out of her pew and knelt beside him. Andy was pleased to see her perform such an act. To his knowledge, it was the first time she had done so. She genuflected and crossed herself, which Andy found astonishing, since he hadn't even known she was familiar with Anglican rituals. She was kneeling very close to him. He kept his head down, continuing to pray for his family and his for all of those who resided at Winthrop Manor.

Estelle's hand slowly made its way toward Andy. His eyes were tightly closed and he wasn't aware of the movement. Then, in a swift motion, she placed her hand on the crotch of his pants.

Andy leaped up, pulling away, completely dumbfounded. His eyes flew open, and he looked at Estelle's face.

Her eyes were closed, but she was not praying.

"Estelle!" He grabbed hold of her hand. "What in God's name do you think you're doing?" His voice echoed in the silent chapel.

She looked innocently towards him. "People like to be touched there. I was trying to make you happy," she chirped.

"Estelle, don't ever, ever do that again. Not to me and not to anyone else. That is a wicked, disgusting thing to do. Who told you such a thing?"

"Father Comer," she responded.

"Father Comer?" Andy echoed. He was the new vicar assigned to the Winthrop-on-Hart church, who also conducted Sunday services in the Winthrop Manor chapel. Andy was in complete shock.

"Yes," Estelle answered. "We meet here regularly. A friend told me all about the difference between boys and girls, and she said that everybody likes being touched. I tried it with Father Comer, and he loved it. Now he lets me do that whenever we're alone."

"Oh, my dear God in heaven! A man of the cloth, no less. Estelle, I'm ashamed of you. I'm equally ashamed of the vicar. I hope you realize that I am going to have to tell Mummy."

"Oh, Andy, don't do that. You'll only get me into trouble—and the vicar too. He told me it was very wrong, but he said he couldn't help himself."

"My dear. He *can* help himself. He obviously has little self-control, and on top of that, he's taking advantage of you."

"Well… I think maybe I'm taking advantage of him," Estelle said with a giggle and the immoral look that only she was occasionally able to get in her eyes. "My friend says I seduced him."

"What in the world is the matter with you, Estelle? These are the sorts of things your mother, Elisabeth, and Tom have told me about you, but I've always stood up for you. I couldn't imagine a young lady your age even having such thoughts, but you've just proven what they've told me is true. That's apparently the reason Tom and Elisabeth took Susan and moved back to Cloverdale. You frighten me, Estelle. Come with me this minute. First, we're going to have a talk with Mum. Then, we are going to have a conversation with Vicar Comer."

He grabbed Estelle's hand and literally dragged her down the center aisle of the chapel and out of the massive, double doors. By then, Estelle was screaming at the top of her lungs and holding her legs rigid, so Andy had to pull her with all his might. Finally, he simply picked her up and carried her the remaining distance to the manor. They entered the front doors. Andy prayed his mother would be in the great hall, but she was not. He called her name, and she answered from the area above the stairway, in the gallery which overlooked the hall. Andy continued to carry the unruly Estelle up the stairway, until he was standing in front of Josephine. She looked appalled when she saw Estelle thrown over Andy's shoulder, kicking and screaming.

"What in God's name is going on here?" she shouted.

"I apologise, Mother, but this is the only way I could make certain I was able to bring her to you. I've just made a disgusting find."

"Oh, Lord. What now?" Josephine asked.

"I was kneeling, saying a prayer in the chapel. Estelle asked to accompany me. Of course, I had no difficulty with such a request. However, as I knelt, she knelt beside me, reached over and placed her hand on—well, on my crotch. I absolutely could not believe it."

"Estelle. What in the world? Where would you even dream up such a filthy idea?" her mother asked.

"There's nothing the matter with it," answered Estelle. "My friend taught it to me. She told me it feels good." Her face contorted into the malicious sneer that Josephine and the others had become used to. "Father Comer likes it," she added.

"Estelle! Are you saying that you and the vicar are…" Josephine couldn't bring herself to say another word?

"Well, to be honest, we do quite a bit of cuddling. It feels very good."

Josephine couldn't help herself. She drew her hand back and slapped Estelle across the face. "So, you are the one who initiates this behaviour, Estelle. It's shocking that a vicar would use his power to do such a thing, but men are very vulnerable. I have a suspicion you know that."

"Umm. I guess I do," she grinned. "I watched Uncle Tom and Aunt Elisabeth one time while I was standing behind the cupboard in their room. I asked the vicar if we could do that, but he said we would need to wait a bit until

I'm older. So, we do a lot of touching and cuddling. He kept repeating that it was very wrong and a sin against God, but he didn't stop me."

Andy stood beside his mother with a look of pure horror on his face. "I now believe everything you've told me about Estelle, Mother. Something has to be done. To begin with, Father Comer will have to go."

"I *do* think he deserves the presumption of innocence, Andy, given Estelle's history of dishonesty. I agree completely however, that if what she says is true, he will have to be sent from his post at Winthrop-on-Hart," answered Josephine. "But that isn't the only change that's going to take place. Estelle is going to be sent to an extremely strict school. Perhaps a place like that can put some values into her sinful mind. God knows we've all tried, to no avail. I know of a school in Kent, and I intend to contact them immediately."

"I think that's an excellent idea, Mum," Andy answered.

Estelle began to scream at the top of her lungs. "You are not going to send me to some stupid school. I shall refuse to go. I'll tell the authorities that Andy took off my knickers and—took advantage of me!" she finished.

"Oh, you horrid, little creature!" shouted Andy. "You'll do no such thing."

At precisely that moment, Elisabeth appeared in the same area accompanied by Susan. "What in the world is going on here?" she enquired. "I can hear your voices all the way to my bedchamber."

❧

Andy, Josephine, and Estelle stood staring at one another. Finally, Estelle spoke with a truly malevolent gleam in her eye. "I know that Oliver is my father, and I know that you killed him. I also know about Radcliffe and Uncle Tom burying him in the back of our grounds here at Winthrop Manor. I hid behind a door one time and overheard you talking to Aunt Elisabeth. I'm going to tell the men from Scotland Yard everything I know. You will all go to prison for murder!" Estelle screamed.

Josephine's face turned white. "Estelle, since you think you know so much, perhaps you are also aware that Oliver raped me and that you are the product of that rape," Josephine said between clenched teeth. They were words she had never meant to speak, and the guilt was overwhelming. However, the situation had become totally untenable.

Estelle ran at Josephine with her head lowered. She rammed her body straight into her mother's abdomen, knocking her backwards. Estelle jumped on top of her mother and began to pummel her with fists which seemed stronger than they should for her age.

Josephine rolled out of the way, but Estelle jumped on her mother again, continuing to strike her. Suddenly, Josephine reached the top of the stairway and began to tumble rapidly, followed by Estelle who could find nothing to break the fall. The two bodies toppled head over heels down the lengthy, winding staircase.

When they reached the marble floor in the Great Hall, there was a sickening thud. There was no sign of movement from either mother or daughter. Andy ran to the telephone and called for the local ambulance. He knelt beside his mother, feeling for a heartbeat. There was definitely quite a sound pulse. He breathed a sigh of relief, and prayed that help would soon arrive.

At the same time, Elisabeth ran to Estelle. She also found a pulsation, but the child was whimpering. It was clear that she was in pain.

A siren sounded in the distance. The ambulance had arrived. Josephine drifted in and out of consciousness. In a moment of lucidity, she glanced over at her daughter's form, which lay not far from her own. She *did* appear to be breathing, but her body was sprawled at an odd angle. Had Estelle's neck or back been damaged?

In a matter of minutes, two ambulance attendants reached them. One rushed to Josephine's side and took her pulse. "Are you able to speak?" he asked.

"Yes. It hurts to breathe, though." She pointed to the area above her abdomen.

He examined her and said that he suspected she had broken some ribs. She also told him she had a violent headache. He said they would transport her to hospital, and would attempt to discover if she had suffered a concussion.

The other attendant examined Estelle. She was now completely silent. "Where do you hurt?" He didn't know if she would or could answer.

"I cannot feel my legs. My back is totally numb. So are my arms."

"Can you tell me what happened here?" asked the man tending Josephine.

Suddenly, Estelle found her voice, and it was quite strong. "Yes! My mother pushed me down the stairs, and she fell too, after trying to grab hold of the banister."

"Why would your mother have done that?" he asked.

"Because she tried to break up an argument between my brother and me."

"What was the argument about?"

"A long time ago, I overheard my mother and my aunt saying that my real father was my uncle Oliver. He was my mum's husband's brother. Mum was having an affaire with him. When my other uncle, Dr. Tom Drew, found out the truth, he killed my father. Our butler, Radcliffe and Uncle Tom, buried my father in the woods. All of them should be in prison. My mother, my uncle, and our butler. Also, Mum discovered that I'm in love with the local vicar, Father Comer, and that he loves me too. She was furious. That's why she pushed me down the stairs."

Each adult looked astounded. A grow man—a vicar-interested in a seven-year-old! It was unthinkable. On top of that there had been signs that Hope Reed and the Vicar were attracted toward each other.

Josephine overheard this entire conversation. It was beyond belief. The worst part of the entire tale was that Scotland Yard would undoubtedly search the property looking for Oliver's body. Fear caused her to tremble uncontrollably. She was absolutely certain, of course, that Scotland Yard was not about to believe a vicar would be interested in a seven-year-old.

"We'll report these findings to Scotland Yard, but at this moment it's our job to transport the two of you to hospital," said the gentleman who was treating Estelle. Josephine and her daughter were lifted onto gurneys and carried out to the waiting ambulances.

Before they departed, Andy stood on the steps of Winthrop Manor and held up a hand. It was quite obvious that this was not a life and death matter and he was not about to let his out-of-control sister get away with the lies she had told. Tom, Elisabeth, Radcliffe and Mrs. Shellady were also present. They'd all overheard the lies Estelle had told.

"Gentlemen, I know you are in a rush. Nevertheless, I want it clearly understood that what you have just heard from my younger sister is a pack of lies. There is a modicum of truth, but the accident that took place in the last half hour did not happen the way you were told. My mother *did not* push my sister down the stairway. When you speak to Scotland Yard, please make certain that they are aware that I am a witness to the entire scene and can tell them precisely what occurred. I am the Earl of Winthrop. I would hope my word would carry more weight than that of a mere child with a wretched history of lying.

14

Josephine and Estelle were hospitalised. As the ambulance attendants had suspected, Josephine had suffered a concussion although it was not severe. She also had several broken ribs that were taped tightly.

Estelle had a much more serious injury, but it wasn't life threatening. The worst was spinal trauma. Her back was not broken, nor her neck as Josephine had feared. However, she *had* suffered a ruptured disc that would require surgery as well as months of recuperation. Josephine was so intensely infuriated at Estelle's lies about the accident and her recitation of erroneous facts surrounding Oliver's death, that she scarcely cared what her daughter's condition was.

Just as Josephine feared, the local constable appeared in her room at hospital shortly after she was settled. She'd had no opportunity to speak with Radcliffe, Tom, Elisabeth, Andy, or Roderick—which placed her in an awkward position. Had they been able to compare stories it would have been far easier to undergo questioning by the police. She thought the situation through and made a firm decision to tell the truth. It was the only thing to do. She had lived long enough to learn that when one told a lie, it only created more difficulty. The constable was accompanied by another man who introduced himself as the Chief Inspector for Winthrop-on-Hart.

"Lady Josephine, we're sorry to disturb you so quickly after your accident. However, we received information from the ambulance attendants that's rather upsetting. It *does* require investigation."

"I understand," Josephine replied. "I was present when my daughter told her outrageous lies. I heard everything she said. I'm more than happy to set the record straight."

Both men introduced themselves. "I am Chief Inspector Ian Stephens," the older of the two stated. "This is my right-hand man, Constable Earnest Parker. We need to ask you some questions."

"Yes, of course," Josephine murmured. "Please continue."

❧

The chief inspector began. "You indicate that you overheard what your daughter said. Is her name Estelle?"

"Indeed, I did," Josephine answered. "Yes, her name is Estelle."

"You also say that they are lies. Can you please elaborate?"

"I'll be happy to. You see, my late husband, the Earl of Winthrop, was killed in an auto accident in London at the end of April, nineteen-twenty-five. He had a brother, whose name was Oliver. Oliver had been serving time in Wandsworth Prison for kidnapping our son while my husband was serving in the British Expeditionary Forces. Rather than go into all of those details, I'm sure your office has all of the records pertaining to that particular crime. Anyway, Oliver was granted compassionate leave from prison to attend my husband's funeral. I wasn't told of this and was shocked when I saw him at the reception following the services. The reception was held at our home, Winthrop Manor."

Josephine rearranged herself in the hospital bed, as her ribs were hurting. Then, she continued. "I was appalled when I saw him there. He was a despicable human being. To be honest, I was somewhat concerned that he would find a way to escape, thereby not returning to prison. However, he assured me that he'd been escorted to the funeral by a detective from Scotland Yard. Be that as it may, he *did* manage to elude the detective, steal a car from our garages, and disappear. Scotland Yard believed he was headed for London, where he could board a train to any number of ports, and escape to either America. Canada, or Australia. They assured me I had nothing to be concerned about." Josephine coughed and took a sip of water.

"Unfortunately, they were mistaken. Oliver appeared in my room that night after the lights were turned down. Without going into too much detail, it should suffice to say that he had a knife in his hand and proceeded to sexually assault me. Of course, I was in shock. In the melee that ensued, during the rape, I managed to get my hands on the knife. When he rolled off my body, I stabbed him in the back several times, as well as his side and his groin. I killed him. Not only that, gentlemen, *I would do so again.*"

The men looked exceedingly uncomfortable. "Is what your daughter said true? Did you become pregnant with her as a result of this alleged assault?"

Josephine's face tuned beet red. "I am offended by your use of the word 'alleged.' What I suffered at his hands was the worst experience of my Life. He deserved everything he got."

"We apologise, your Ladyship, but until the facts of a case are proven, we must use correct terminology," replied the chief inspector.

"Yes, well the correct terminology would be *rape*, gentlemen. *Rape*. I am the proof. So is Estelle. Do you understand what rape is?"

"Yes, certainly. It's just that Estelle states that she overheard you speaking to your sister-in-law, Mrs. Drew, about having had an affair with Mr Oliver."

"My daughter is a pathological liar. She inherited the trait from her disgusting father. While it sounds abysmally harsh, I wish she had never been born. She has brought nothing but heartache from the moment she entered this world. Interrogate the staff at Winthrop Manor. You'll not find one person who doesn't tell you what I've just recounted about Estelle."

"We definitely intend do so, madam. Can you explain why his murder wasn't reported to the authorities?"

"Yes, it was at my request. My husband loved Winthrop Manor It has been in the family for generations. It meant more to him almost more than anything else in his life— besides me and our son, Andrew. I was not about to put a stain on the reputation of that splendid home. Members of the aristocracy can be mean, spiteful people. Had they heard that a murder had taken place at Winthrop Manor, within a week all of England would have been buzzing with the news. I'd just lost my husband. I was not going to allow such a thing to happen. The newspaper men would have flooded our property. I had been through quite enough. It was an easy decision to make. My brother-in-law, Dr. Tom Drew—who is married to my late husband's sister, Elisabeth—and our butler, Radcliffe, felt it should be reported to the authorities. I overruled them. I asked Radcliffe and Tom to bury Oliver's body on our property, and bless their hearts, they complied."

"Are you able to tell us precisely who and how many people were on the premises the night of the...assault?"

"Let me see." Josephine counted on her fingers. "Of course, I was present; along with the Winthrop Manor staff headed by Radcliffe, our long-time butler; Mrs. Shellady, the housekeeper; Mrs. Boyle, the cook; and myriad other serving people, footmen, under-cooks, parlour maids, and the like. Emma, my lady's maid, was also on the premises. In addition, there was our retired cook, Vera Whitaker, who is now suffering from dementia, and Winnie Lawrence, the companion who was hired to care for her. Then, in terms of family members, there was my son, Andrew; my brother- and sister-in-law, Dr. Tom and Elisabeth Drew. We had invited Father Sebastian Comer, the local vicar, who had performed the services for my beloved husband, to stay for an overnight visit, so he was in a guest suite. I believe all were at Winthrop Manor on that ghastly day and night."

"May I ask one more question?" the inspector enquired.

The two men had seemed somewhat startled at Josephine's blunt honesty. "We *do* appreciate everything you've told us," the inspector said. "Of course, we have more interviews to conduct. Your candid recitation of events should be an enormous help. We *will* want to send a team out to unearth the victim's remains. Have we your permission to do so?"

"Absolutely," Josephine agreed. "Dr. Drew and Radcliffe can lead you to the proper place."

"Have you any objection to our speaking to your daughter, Estelle? She *is* under age and will require parental consent to be interviewed."

"Interview her to your hearts' content. I only ask that you be quite skeptical of anything she says."

The detectives did not respond to Josephine's warning. "Thank you, Lady Josephine. We do wish you a speedy recovery and undoubtedly will see you again. Scotland Yard will be involved in the case too, but there doesn't appear to be any need for them to interview you until your discharge from hospital."

"Elisabeth and I stayed up the remainder of the night, during which the murder took place, scrubbing my bedroom of the copious amounts of blood. I think all of my information covers what took place quite thoroughly."

After the two men left the room, Josephine considered asking if a telephone could be brought to her room, but she was certain such a request would not be honoured, primarily because it was probably impossible. She wondered if Radcliffe, Elisabeth, Tom, and Roderick would tell the truth, as she had.

They didn't. Radcliffe tried to take the blame for the murder. He told the authorities he'd heard a commotion in Josephine's suite and had gone to her door. Instead of knocking, he said that he'd opened it and found Oliver in the midst of the assault. He went on to say that *he* had collected the knife when Oliver dropped it on the floor beside the bed in his sexual fervor and had committed the murder. He further said that it was he alone who had buried Oliver.

Tom said that he and his wife had known nothing about the entire affair until Josephine came to them about her pregnancy. It was an obvious attempt to protect Elisabeth.

Roderick told the truth, as he knew it. He related the conversation he'd had with his niece after the awful assault was over. The old man *did* say that he totally believed Josephine, and that he'd never in his life known her to lie.

That left Estelle. She held firm to her original story. The girl could act so exasperatingly innocent. By the time she was interrogated, it was Scotland Yard who conducted the interview. Her wide open, green eyes with tears streaming from them made it difficult for the authorities not to believe her—especially when all other witnesses' stories didn't match. Since by that time, the vicar's name had been brought into the picture, he too was brought in for questioning.

The poor man was unbelievably embarrassed. No one could blame him. He was young and extremely good-looking. Having graduated from Cambridge and then the London University School of Theology, he had only recently been given his first assignment as Vicar of St. Luke's Anglican Church in Winthrop-on-Hart. He had quite blond hair and intensely pale blue eyes. In addition, he was tall with a masculine build. His smile was said to attract a great many of the women in the village who had previously been Catholics but had chosen to be confirmed as Anglicans the moment Father Comer arrived on the scene. His name was Sebastian Comer. He was unmarried. Of course, Anglican Vicars *are allowed* to marry—unlike Catholic priests. Undoubtedly many young ladies hoped to win his love. It was difficult for the investigators to believe that Father Comer could possibly have become enamoured with Estelle.

"Father Comer, is there any truth to the story given by Lady Estelle regarding her activities with you in the chapel?" Inspector Secrest asked.

"Sir, I haven't heard her recitation of the facts as she presented them, so I cannot say with certainty. However, if she has given you information implying that I was in some way sexually interested in her, of course the answer is rubbish."

Inspector Secrest raised his brow. "She *did* imply such a thing. I must also tell you that she was very explicit with the details she presented."

"That doesn't necessarily surprise me. I'm sorry to be so blunt, but in my own opinion, there is something ghastly wrong with that young lady. I'm aware that she is cognizant of much more than the average girl her age about sexual matters. I can also tell you that she is a fearful liar. I *am* well-acquainted with her. It would be difficult for me not to be. She shows up in my office at the church nearly every afternoon. In the beginning, I made honest attempts to be kind to her. I presumed she had some sort of problem and felt the need to discuss it with me. She was so young, it seemed unlikely that it could be anything serious, although one never knows. However, that wasn't her purpose in visiting me."

"What was her purpose, Father?"

"It is my suspicion that she had it in her mind to lure me. Believe me, that would have been absolutely impossible. Obviously, she is only a child. I cannot imagine where a young lady that age could possibly have the thoughts which I suspect she did, indeed, have."

"She is seven years of age, Father. Men have been known to become involved with girls that age."

"Not *this* man, Inspector. I take my vows seriously and *certainly* didn't spend all of the years I did studying theology to throw away my chance to be a vicar. I am *not* a pervert, if that is what you are implying, and I don't mind telling you that I resent your words."

"What gave you the notion that Lady Estelle was of a mind to seduce you?"

"Initially, she directly asked if I wore knickers under my vestment. I don't recall ever being so shocked. She continued by making a request to put her hand underneath my cassock. Of course, I told her no in an exceptionally strong voice. *The girl is evil.* I do not make use of that word frequently. I am an Anglican, not a Catholic. I do not believe in exorcism. However, this young lady—and I use the word *lady* advisedly—is *greatly* troubled. I know the family, and they are fine people. I understand, however, that she has made an assertion that her true father was the Earl of Winthrop's brother, whom I never knew. His name was Oliver, and according to Estelle, her mother had an affaire with him. I *highly* doubt the truth of such a statement. Lady Josephine, as I understand, denies this with all of her heart and swears that Oliver raped her. She is one of the finest ladies I have ever had the pleasure to know. Oliver was serving time in prison on kidnapping charges from what I have heard. The rape accusation makes much more sense to me."

Father Comer reached up and scratched his head. He then excused himself, taking a sip of water. "If indeed it *is* true that Oliver is Estelle's biological father, perhaps she takes after him. I am not a physician, nor a person well-versed in that field of study known as psychology. It might be valuable for you to interview such an individual."

The detectives took notes during the entire interview. Later, both were inclined to believe everything Father Comer had said. They considered his advice regarding an interview with someone trained in psychology. However, they were personally unfamiliar with anyone of that sort. Both had heard the name Sigmund Freud, undoubtedly the most well-known individual in that field. Unfortunately, he did not live in Great Britain but in Austria.

The men were so intrigued with the prospect that this revolutionary field of medicine might hold a key to the case they were investigating, they decided to enquire about the possibility of such a professional practicing in Great Britain. Their investigation led them to Maudsley Hospital in London, which had a small division dedicated to Child Psychiatry. When the Maudsley Hospital opened in February 1923, that small department for the treatment of children under Dr. D. W. Dawson began its operation. The detectives learned that the first physicians who worked in the children's department at The Maudsley employed a wide array of practical approaches to the treatment of mental illness in children. They ranged from dream interpretation and dietary supplements, to drug treatment and sensory deprivation.

On admission to The Maudsley, every child was administered a thorough physical examination. An account of the child's early history, particularly noting any traumas or shocks to the nervous system in the form of frights, major injuries, or infections was conducted. Any signs of mental illness in relatives were also a cause for concern due to the theory of hereditary transmission.

The decision was made to have Estelle thoroughly evaluated at the institution. She was brought to London by her mother, Lady Josephine, and was put through the extremely thorough protocol. Aside from the possibility that she had inherited traits from her biological father, the personnel who evaluated her *did* question whether the child had ever been sexually abused.

Josephine was horrified. "Of course, nothing of the sort has *ever* taken place at Winthrop Manor," she stated with anger in her voice.

"We simply have to ask any question that might be relevant to the result of test interpretations," one of the physicians replied.

Most children referred to The Maudsley came from working-class homes. Many lived in squalid conditions. They were usually noted as being in poor general health and were often malnourished. This was certainly *not* the case with Estelle. It was also discovered that the majority of children studied at The Maudsley were expected to carry out household tasks at home and as a result, didn't attend school regularly. Those who *were* at school were often well below the general school standards.

Again, this was not the situation with Estelle. In fact, her grades had always been superior to those of her classmates, and education had been stressed in her home, beginning with her nanny. In several cases, it was discovered that adults or older siblings who were supposed to be caring for the children had sexually assaulted them. After speaking with Josephine, they were convinced that there was absolutely no evidence of such a thing having occurred in the Winthrop case.

It was finally determined by a team of physicians that there had been substantial alteration in Estelle's behaviour since early 1930, when she was four. Violent temper tantrums, screaming, kicking and swearing, as well as sneaking about, inappropriate interest in sexual matters, extreme lying, depression, and violent behaviour at times. All had been displayed at various times. She had also demonstrated aggression towards other children. The doctors also noted nail biting, antagonism to her family—especially Josephine, Susan, and Aunt

Elisabeth, which was followed by extreme, prolonged sobbing. Josephine couldn't help but be aware that this would have been the time when Estelle had learned that Oliver was her father. Was she responsible for Estelle's repugnant behavior, because she had blurted out the truth about the rape? She did not mention that incident to the professionals at The Maudsley, and their conclusion was that while all of the child's behaviour was interesting, none led to any sort of specific diagnosis other than that she suffered from a "behavioural disorder of unknown origin."

Anglican services were held each Sunday in the chapel at Winthrop Manor with Father Comer officiating. After they were over, he was always invited to share the noon dinner at Winthrop Manor. Nannies were never treated as other members of the staff, and Hope had always been invited to participate in the Sunday repast. Those occasions grew in importance for both her and the vicar.

After the lovely noonday dinner was finished, Father Comer and Hope had begun to enjoy a stroll in the gardens on warm days or have a conversation by the drawing room fire in colder instances. They had begun to look forward to such meetings. One night, after prolonged weeks, the two found themselves seated side-by-side sipping delicious, freshly brewed tea following the evening meal.

"Sebastian," Hope asked. "Have you reached a conclusion about this wicked investigation regarding Estelle?"

"Not completely. As I stated at the outset, I remain quite fearful in my belief that Estelle is utterly immoral. The entire episode appears to stem from both Estelle and her father being outright evil. My reasoning may sound rather simple, but it's truly the only explanation that makes any sense."

"I tend to agree with you," murmured Hope. "It's all been so terribly vile. What do you suppose will come of the investigation?"

"In the end, it is beyond my conception that Lady Josephine or anyone else could be found responsible for murder."

Hope shivered. "What an ugly word."

"Yes, it is. Unfortunately, we live in an unpleasant world at times," he replied. "Still, I believe it will be resolved in the end. I shouldn't worry unnecessarily."

"I know, and I'm making every effort not to. However, if I'm honest, the matter is never far from my mind."

"I understand," he replied. "That's only natural."

"I'm truly thankful that I've had you throughout this nightmare. You cannot know the solace you've brought."

"Thank you. That means a lot to me. Er, not to change the subject, but at some time in the future does the possibility exist that you might agree to walk out for an evening with me? I thought perhaps we might dine somewhere and take in a film?"

"Oh, Sebastian, of course. I'd love that. How thoughtful of you.'

"The honour would be all mine." He smiled and his intense blue eyes held a glow.

"We'll set a date sometime very soon," she said. "It's been so long since something of this nature has presented itself."

"Quite," he answered. "What would you think of next Saturday?"

"Perfect."

He pulled her close to him on the sofa. "I feel I must say what I'm thinking. You've made me very happy."

She stared into his extraordinary eyes, and after only a few seconds they kissed. Not a passionate kiss but not brotherly either. "I care for you a good deal. Am I frightening you with such a declaration?"

"No, I feel precisely the same way."

He kissed her again. "I anticipate something wonderful resulting from our friendship," he whispered.

"Yes. Yes, so do I."

15

❧❧

After Estelle was released from hospital, everyone at Winthrop Manor hoped and prayed they would see a change in the girl. Unfortunately, their prayers went unanswered. She had healed quite nicely in spite of her rather serious wounds, but she walked with a slight stoop caused from the spinal injury. The physicians *did* hold out hope for further improvement. There had been also been fervent anticipation that the analysis at Maudsley might have uncovered the reason for her unseemly behaviour. However, it had not done so.

Nothing stopped her usual malevolent, vicious behaviour. The girl had an uncanny ability to sense what was happening in the house even before a word had been spoken. The only time she appeared to act normally was when she spent time with Andy, Vera, or Winnie. Andy was, of course, not at home often, and now even he no longer believed that she was the product of stories that the family invented. Thus, Josephine decided to talk with Vera and her companion, Winnie, regarding Estelle.

She knocked on Vera's apartment door and Winnie opened it. Josephine smiled, as she was invited into the attractive rooms where Vera spent the majority of her time. "Winnie, I need to speak with Vera, alone, if you don't have any objection," Josephine said.

"Certainly not, Lady Josephine. I'm sure Mrs. Whitaker would love to spend some time with you. I'll make my way downstairs to the kitchen and visit with Mrs. Boyle. Please summon me when you require my presence." With that, Winnie exited the rooms.

Vera was sitting by the large window overlooking the fountains and gardens behind Winthrop Manor.

Josephine reached out and took both of Vera's hands in hers. "How are you feeling today? It's lovely to see you."

"Oh, Lady Josephine. Yes, it's always splendid to see you," replied Vera. "I so enjoy company. I wish Win would visit more often. Is he awfully busy with his duties now that he is the earl?"

Josephine had to struggle to hold back tears. Win had been Vera's most beloved member of the family. Obviously, she no longer remembered that he'd lost his life. Josephine would never have done or said anything to sadden Vera, so she simply nodded in reply.

"I'm so happy that Estelle visits me frequently," Vera continued. "She is a lovely girl."

"Yes, well, it's Estelle whom I wish to speak with you about, Vera. She appears to be extremely fond of you, and yet the rest of the household finds her very difficult to deal with."

"Oh no," Vera nearly shouted. "Estelle is a wonderful girl. She is so filled with questions about life. I'm happy to be the person she comes to for answers. I feel like a grandmother to her."

"What sort of questions? What sort of answers?" Josephine frowned.

"Oh, the sort all girls ask at her age," Vera answered.

"I'm not certain I understand," Josephine remarked. "Can you be more specific?"

"I can't recall right now. Perhaps they will come to me. I find that I can't remember things like I once did."

"Yes, well, we all tend to get that way as we grow older," said Josephine.

"It *does* seem to me that she wanted to know about the things men and women do and how babies are made."

"Can you remember how old she was when she asked such questions?" Josephine commented.

"Not off hand, Miss Josephine. Awhile ago, I'm thinking."

"That would mean she was awfully young. She's only seven now. That seems quite young to be interested in such matters. However, you don't know exactly what her questions were?"

"Um, well perhaps. I think she wanted to know why men and women would do—oh you know—the thing that causes babies."

"Yes. It's called *intercourse*, Vera."

"Yes, I guess so."

"Do you remember your answer to her question?"

Vera smiled, and looked happy. "Yes. I *do* remember." She seemed very proud of herself for her recall. "I told her that people do it because it feels good."

Josephine was horrified but knew she should never let Vera know how she felt. The only thing she could think to say was, "I see."

"Yes, that was my answer. That *is* why people do it, isn't it? Estelle needed to know. Now she does."

Josephine chatted a bit more, but she had a strong need to remove herself from Vera's presence. Could Vera have contributed to Estelle's sinful behaviour? This troublesome thought skimmed through Josephine's mind. She rang the bell to send for Winnie. The companion returned promptly. Josephine stopped her at the doorway, as she was about to leave.

"Winnie, before I leave, I need to ask you something," Josephine said.

"Yes, of course, milady. How may I be of help?"

"I've been having a good deal of trouble with Estelle for a long time now. I won't go into all the details, but she does not behave in a ladylike manner and disobeys nearly everything she is instructed to do. At one time, Estelle was a good student and a sweet child. Then, we all began to see a great change come over her. I'd like your impression, Winnie. I know she spends a lot of time with you and Vera."

"Oh milady, no. Estelle is a perfect angel when she's with Vera and me. She *did* once hint that she'd found out that your husband's brother was her *true* father. I had no idea if that could be true or not. You know how children can get strange ideas into their heads sometimes. She showed some anger about it, I remember that. But she didn't mention it again."

"I cannot imagine where she would have come up with such a thought." The fact that Estelle knew the truth frightened Josephine immensely. Her memory returned to the physicians who had analyzed Estelle at The Maudsley. Was that why Estelle's behaviour had changed so abruptly? Should Josephine have told her the truth long ago? If she had found out the truth, had it affected her psychologically? Josephine suddenly felt sick, claustrophobic. She had to take deep breaths and thought she might faint.

"Well, I must go," she said. "Thank you for that information. Perhaps I need to have a talk with Estelle." She quickly opened the door and exited.

Almost immediately upon Josephine's return from the Winthrop-on-Hart Station, where she'd held her beloved son in her arms, bidding him farewell, as he departed for Oxford, there was more trouble involving Estelle. Whenever Andy left, Josephine experienced terrible anxiety. As she entered the doors of Winthrop Manor, angry voices drifted from the second level. Hope was tearfully shouting at Estelle. Sobs were emanating from the nanny's voice, and she sounded at her wit's end.

"Now, what has happened?" Josephine yelled, as she ran up the stairway. "I needn't ask who is involved. Estelle, what have you done?"

Before the girl had an opportunity to launch into another of her tales, Josephine approached her, placing a hand in front of her face. "I want the truth, Estelle. I'm completely fed up with you and your abysmal lies."

"As usual, you won't believe me!" Estelle screamed. "I walked into what I thought was an empty room—the yellow guest room—searching for a book. As I opened the doorway, the Vicar Howe and Miss Reed were on top of the counterpane on the bed. Both were very mussed up. They looked surprised when they saw me, and sat up, brushing off their clothes."

Both Vicar Howe and Hope Reed were standing beside Estelle Hope placed her head in her hands. "Oh Estelle, where *do* you come up with such lies?"

The vicar's face assumed a dark expression. "Estelle! You *will* apologize to your aunt immediately. This is not going to continue." He turned to Josephine. "Lady Josephine, I refuse to stand here and listen to slurs made toward this lovely woman. I might as well tell you that I find myself very much in love with Hope. She tells me that she reciprocates my feelings. It is my intention to join up with the military. I'll be serving as a chaplain. I also fully intend to make Hope my bride before I leave for training. Until such time, I do not intend to hear another word out of this vile creature." He pointed toward Estelle. "You know as well as I do that Hope is as virtuous as a newborn lamb. Estelle, you, on the other hand, have a filthy mind and frankly, I find you repulsive."

There was dead silence in the room. Vicar Comer had finally spoken the words that so many others had wished so say aloud for such a long time. Josephine quickly made up her mind that the best way to handle the situation would be to make a request for Estelle to remove herself from their presence. Then, the remaining members of the family could continue with a celebratory atmosphere in honour of the vicar and Hope.

"Estelle. Go to your room. I shall come and speak with you in a few minutes. In the meantime, I want you to think about your latest behaviour. I also want you to know that there are going to be some major changes in your life. I don't know if you thought you would be allowed to continue this abominable behaviour forever, but you cannot and will not."

Josephine turned her back on her daughter, folding Hope in her arms. "My dear, this is joyful news. I absolutely cannot think of two people better suited to one another than you and Sebastian Comer. From the moment I saw the two of you standing next to one another I thought that. With all of the sadness and upset over the Great War this brings happiness into our lives. Do, please, tell me that you'll agree to be married at the Winthrop Manor Chapel."

Hope's eyes filled with tears. "Do you mean it, milady?" She turned to Father Comer. "Sebastian, how would you feel about that?"

"I can't think of anything I'd like more. We can have the assistant rector perform the ceremony. You know him—Reverend Stoddard."

"Yes, of course. I like him. We won't have a large wedding, will we?" Hope asked.

"Not extravagant, but I *do* think all parishioners should receive an invitation. Obviously, all family as well," Sebastian suggested.

"I'm all undone. I don't know what to say or how to thank you," Hope exclaimed.

"Then let's definitely plan on it."

"Not unless significant changes take place," murmured Hope.

A major decision was reached regarding Estelle during the following week. Josephine had a long discussion with Uncle Roderick, followed by another talk with Tom and Elisabeth. All unanimously concluded that the time had arrived to send Estelle away to boarding school. The difficulty lay with locating a school that would be willing to accept her. She seemed awfully young to be sent away to board, although it was not unheard of. The family discussed the dilemma, and decided upon initiating a search for a well-run school specialising in troubled young ladies. It would not be an easy project. There were many institutions targeting young ladies her age, but few specialised in girls of Estelle's temperament. She had a long history of unsavory behaviour. While the primary reason for the school's existence would need to be concentration upon an applicant's past behaviour, Josephine suspected that there would be few girls whose records could rival Estelle's lengthy list of misdeeds.

Hope and Josephine left Winthrop Manor on a late summer morning, with David driving them in the Rolls Royce. They were armed with a list of schools which Andy had sent to them. It was a truly, lovely day. They had considered taking Estelle with them but reached the conclusion that it would be wiser to first inspect the various schools on their own. After narrowing them down, they would take her with them on a second search.

The Winthrop family was known for its wealth and prestige. However, that didn't necessarily mean that Lady Estelle had a better opportunity for admission to a first-rate school. Tom was able to offer Estelle an advantage, however, because as a physician he was familiar with schools of this sort— schools that were generally classified as both medical facilities and rural boarding schools. They all had first-rate educational staff and equally prominent individuals trained in the very latest psycho-sociology theories. Most were run along country house lines.

Tom was well-acquainted with most every administrator in this sort of institute. Nearly all implemented curricula commensurate with the finest schools of higher learning in Great Britain combined with therapeutic methods of study, such as art and music, creative writing, group discussion delving into personality disorders, and theories of prominent names in the field of neuro-psychiatry. Very few of these schools failed to concentrate heavily upon horseback riding, which had been found to be one of the better methods for treatment of rebellious students. Each girl would be assigned her own steed for which she was expected to become responsible, and time was set aside daily for equestrian pursuits.

The staff at such institutions consisted of individuals well-trained in the treatment of emotional difficulties, as well as traditional teachers in curricula designed for properly-assigned age groups. The institution that Josephine and Hope became completely enamoured with was located in Wiltshire and was housed in a magnificent, old manor, originally known as The Ashford-Griffin House. It presently was known as The Sanford Institute of Learning for Young Ladies with Troubled Natures. The house, situated in an area of outstanding beauty, had been built in the nineteenth century and was an excellent example of Georgian architecture. The headmaster was Dr. Sanford, a child psychiatrist and educator. It was set in a pretty village called Rowan, surrounded by acres of rolling farmland.

Josephine and Hope were utterly intrigued when they laid eyes upon it. Whether Estelle could be helped by such a charming place with a regimen that seemed tailor-made for someone with her troubled past remained to be seen. Nevertheless, it appeared to be a good place to begin. The two women returned to Winthrop Manor armed with literature and brochures for use in their attempt to coax Estelle into making the school her home for at least a year.

Naturally, Estelle balked. The screaming that ensued was enough to drive the entire household insane. Fortunately, Andy was home from Oxford. He studied pamphlets from the school and raved about it resoundingly to Estelle. Because she'd always shown a bit more affection toward Andy, she calmed down and listened to him. It was not an easy sell, but after lengthy discussion she finally agreed to visit the Sanford Institute with him. Still, she made it exceedingly clear she was not about to commit to attendance unless she found it well-suited in every conceivable way.

Andy held out slim hope, so he decided he would see the school himself. Estelle said she wanted to go with him, so she and Andy piled into the automobile. When they arrived in Wiltshire, Estelle had to admit that the surrounding landscape was pretty. Andy parked the car, and they made their way into the age-old building. After walking through various hallways, they finally discovered the headmaster's office. Andy introduced himself and Estelle and requested that they be shown around the school's premises. He looked extremely handsome dressed in his Oxford blazer, and Estelle secretly felt pride to have him by her side although she would have died rather than admit that she wanted to look around the school.

After an hour of climbing stairways and visiting every nook and cranny, from the girls' sleeping quarters to the dining room and classroom buildings, the two were brought back to the administrator's office. Amazingly, Estelle had not been rude. They were asked to make themselves comfortable in front of the large desk that dominated the office.

"Well, Lady Estelle, have you any question I might be able to answer?" Dr. Sanford asked.

"No, sir. I can't think of anything. I think I like the school, especially the stables."

"Ah, yes. The stables seem to be a hit with all our students," he replied. "Do you ride, Estelle?"

"Yes, sir, I do. It's one of my favourite past times."

"Well," Dr. Sanford responded, "we can either provide you with your own horse, or if you have one at home we do have provisions for you to bring it with you. That would be entirely up to your family."

"How often are girls allowed to ride?" she asked.

"Generally, about two hours a day unless the weather doesn't cooperate. If that happens, we allow you to use the time for other purposes."

"How many girls come here to the school?" Estelle asked.

"We expect enrollment this year to be about seventy young women. Of course, that covers the full twelve years. The first year's class is somewhat larger than the second. That would be girls your age. As I indicated, we cover the entire spectrum of classes from primary school through secondary school. Some girls decide further along in time that they are ready to attend another institution or to return home and study under a tutor or governess. Of course, I, as the head administrator, would give my opinion in such a matter, but naturally parents have the final say. Much depends upon the progress that the child has made. As you saw, the room arrangement is quite nice. Two girls share each room, and then there is a lavatory in between those rooms, so four girls have their own private facilities. Meals are taken on campus. We have quite strict rules regarding the dinner hour. Stockings must be worn, and each girl's legs will be checked for compliance. The meal is served at tables of eight girls. Grace is always said before seats are taken. Correct table manners are expected."

"Are students allowed to see boys?" Estelle enquired.

"At your age, absolutely not. If you should remain with us, you would be allowed to walk out with boys at age sixteen."

Andy watched Estelle carefully from the corner of his eye. He expected scowling and expressions of disapproval but was pleasantly surprised to see her head nod, as though she not only understood, but agreed with the rules.

"So, Lady Estelle. How do you feel about the idea of joining our group of young ladies?" Dr. Sanford asked.

"I think I'd like to join your school," she replied.

Andy was astounded. Dr. Sanford turned in his direction. "So, Lord Winthrop. What is your opinion?"

"I'd very much like to see Estelle give this a try." Turning to Estelle, Andy continued. "Estelle, you *do* understand that you will be expected to follow each and every rule to the letter? There can be no rudeness—no unacceptable comments—absolutely no lies."

"I would try very hard to obey the rules. I'm not happy at home. If I could go horseback riding every day, then I think I can do everything else expected of me."

Andy smiled, stood, and shook the administrator's hand. "Thank you, sir. Our family will wait for a letter of confirmation. In the meantime, Estelle will look forward to the start of a new way of life."

Andy wasn't at all certain that Estelle would comply with the regulations accompanying her new life. He wouldn't have been surprised to have heard from his mother that Estelle had been asked to leave the school. The plan was for her to begin attending The Sanford Institute in September of 1934 and to continue until she was seventeen.

Amazingly, she liked the Sanford Institute from the beginning. The early years were spent learning all of the essentials, such as reading, writing, math, in addition to art therapy, horseback riding, and two hours each day talking with Dr. Sanford.

Estelle made significant progress. She slipped a few times and told a gigantic lie or used an improper word, but those occasions were few and far between. When those incidents occurred she was not punished, but certain privileges were taken away, particular horseback riding. She was assigned a roommate, who was evaluated to ascertain that she and Estelle would be compatible. Her name was Pamela Estes. She was taller than Estelle and not as attractive, but their likes and dislikes were similar. Pamela also came from an aristocratic family and her difficulties were synonymous with Estelle's. They grew to like one another a great deal and continued to room together throughout their duration at the institute. They studied very hard, for the curricula was not easy, but they also had a lot of fun, going for hayrides in the autumn, making ornaments for the school Christmas tree in winter, and building a May Pole, which they decorated in the spring. These were all-school projects where everyone joined in the merrymaking.

In 1939, when she was thirteen and in her sixth year, she was strolling around the lovely grounds of the school, which she often did during her free time. She found herself on a farm whose property adjoined the campus. She relished the lovely landscaping. While savouring the truly breathtaking setting surrounding her, she'd spotted a young man in the distance. At the same time, he lifted his head just before entering a large, red barn. Estelle continued to walk slowly, stopping occasionally to run her hands over the bark of elm, oak, and birch trees. They were plentiful around her.

She'd never been considered beautiful, but she was certainly very pretty. She wore her sandy-coloured hair in a bob. Her most bewitching feature was definitely the lovely eyes she'd inherited from her mother. Fortunately, Oliver had not transmitted his horse-like mouth to his daughter, nor the protruding teeth that had contributed to his over-all unattractive appearance. Estelle's lips were neither Oliver's nor Josephine's. Rather, they were nearly an exact copy of Win's. Oliver's lips were oversized for a man's face—fleshy and feminine in nature. Estelle's were nicely shaped and quite thin. The spinal injury that had caused her to walk with a slight stoop had improved significantly and was barely noticeable, yet her self-esteem was extraordinarily low. It never crossed her mind that the young man she had seen would have any interest in her.

☙❧

Neil Johnston saw very few members of the opposite gender on the farm occupied by him and his parents. Of course, the Sanford Institute was in close proximity to his home, and from time to time he *had* seen young ladies coming and going from the brick building. Still, it never crossed his mind to actually speak to one of them. His parents had warned him on many occasions that he was never to make an attempt to introduce himself. He was a shy boy, and his self-esteem equaled Estelle's.

However, he had absolutely no reason for such low self-regard. He was a tall young man with thick, blond hair and light blue eyes. His skin was tanned due to days spent working out of doors. He had been an above-average student, and his father had hopes that if crops were good and wool output from the sheep substantial, he might find the wherewithal to send Neil on to higher education. Neil considered such talk but a dream. While he had liked school, he loved the farm more. He had no desire to follow any other career.

Having stopped outside of the barn, he found himself mesmerised by the girl he saw in the distance. It was a strange and unusual feeling for him. He'd never kissed a girl nor had he ever come close to having a lady friend. If asked, he couldn't have explained why he felt so intrigued by Estelle.

She, on the other hand, had countless episodes in her past when she'd fabricated tales about matters of a sexual nature, although, truth be told, her experiences were no more extensive than Neil's. She glanced in his direction. Timidly, she smiled. Neil was carrying a milk bucket, which he deposited on the ground by the barn, and slowly began to walk toward her. She stood quietly as he approached. Finally, when they were opposite one another, he reached out his hand, and spoke.

"Hello," he said. "My name is Neil Johnston. I've not seen you near our farm before. Do you attend the Sanford Institute?" His voice quivered.

"Yes," Estelle answered. "I love to take walks about the countryside. Have I intruded upon your property? If so, I apologise. I find myself wandering this way and that. I adore sheep and saw a herd of them in the distance. Are they yours?"

"Yes," Neil answered. "We have sheep, dairy cattle, and even some goats. Most of our land is taken up with crops, however. Would you like to come pet some baby lambs?"

Estelle grinned. "Oh, I'd love to. Where are they?"

Neil ran his hand through his thick hair and responded to her enthusiasm. He reached out his hand again and took hold of hers. "Come, I'll show you. They were only recently born in April." Estelle felt a strange sensation when he touched her. No young man had ever shown interest in her, besides exhibiting a modicum of affection. Together they strolled across to the barn. As they walked together, Estelle began to ask questions about the lambs. "I don't know anything about lambs. I thought they were born in the summertime. I'm surprised you have babies now, in the springtime."

"Some breeds *do* foal during all seasons, but we raise Hampshire sheep. They breed in the early winter, and it usually takes about four and a half months for them to give birth. These were born in April." As the two-young people drew closer to the barn, Estelle could hear soft noises. It was the baby lambs. She spotted them, huddled together, near their mother. Estelle grew ecstatic. "Oh, how absolutely precious! Look at their tiny faces. I've never seen sheep with little black faces, yet their bodies are white."

"Yes. As I said earlier, this breed is known as Hampshires. They're a very old breed, common to this area. They *do* have awfully sweet faces, don't they? Raising sheep is a complicated practice. I've learned a lot about the various breeds and which are best for butchering or for wool."

"Oh, don't tell me about the butchering part. I'll never eat a lamb chop again." Estelle's tone was serious.

Neil laughed. "I don't think you'd make a very good farmer. Where do you live when you aren't at school?" He leaned against the wooden enclosure where the lambs either lay down or poked their noses through the space.

"I live near a small village named Winthrop-on-Hart," she answered.

"Yes, I've heard of it. It's in Hampshire, isn't it? Isn't there an incredible manor house? It's supposed to be one of the finest in all of England, I think."

"Um hum," Estelle nodded. "You're speaking of Winthrop Manor."

"That's it. Is it as magnificent as they say?"

"I suppose so," Estelle replied. "I guess I should admit that Winthrop Manor is my home."

"Are you serious? *You* live at Winthrop Manor? Your family must be very important," Awe tinged Neil's voice. "You act as though you're ashamed to live there. I'd be shouting it from the rooftops."

Estelle scraped the dirt floor with her foot. "My mother is a countess, and my father was the Earl of Winthrop. He's dead though. No, I'm not ashamed. Rather the reverse. My family is rather ashamed of me, I'm afraid. They consider me a constant source of irritation and embarrassment."

Neil looked puzzled. "That seems odd. Why would they feel like that? Surely they love you?"

"I guess. Certainly, you're aware that the Sanford Institute isn't just *any* school. You must know that its sole purpose is remediation of young people who have been a source of difficulty for their families."

At those words, Neil took on a look of discomfort. "Um, well, yes. I knew that. Still, the students over there aren't criminals or the like." He smiled and gave her a quizzical expression.

Estelle couldn't help but laugh. "No, don't worry. I'm not a criminal. I've been sort of hard to live with, I guess. My mum decided the Sanford Institute might do me some good."

"Why are you hard to live with? You seem nice enough to me."

"Oh, I used lie about stuff all of the time. I don't really know why I did that. Sometimes my mother thought the lies I told were the truth. Anyway, to be honest, I *have* done some things that weren't very nice. But, I've been at the school for six years now, and I'm just beginning my seventh. I don't think I act the way I used to anymore."

"Do you ever go home to Winthrop Manor?"

"Oh, yes. I spend Christmas and Easter there and all of the summer. I feel much more comfortable now, since my family doesn't seem afraid of me."

"So, your father is deceased? Are you at all close with your mother?"

"I didn't used to be, but it's better now. It's a complicated story. I used to be close with my brother, Andy, but he decided he didn't think very highly of me anymore either. Maybe someday I'll tell you. That is, if I see you again."

"How old are you?" Neil asked.

"Thirteen. I'll be fourteen in February," she answered.

"I'm seventeen," Neil replied.

She reached down and petted one of the baby lambs. "I think they have such cute faces. Would you care if I came over and watched them grow up?"

"No, not at all. If you didn't live at a school, I'd give you one as a pet. Even though it couldn't live with you, if you wanted, you could pick one out and give it a name. Then it would be yours, and you could come see it as often as you wanted."

"It won't be butchered, will it? I couldn't stand that."

"Nope. These lambs will be used for shearing. So, your lamb will grow up to be a sheep that stays on our farm."

"We have thousands of acres at Winthrop Manor. Do you suppose I could bring my lamb home when I return there someday?"

"Sure. I don't think my mum and dad would mind."

Estelle looked over the litter of black-faced babies carefully. "I think I'd like a girl. Can you show me a little girl?"

"Okay." Neil reached down and plucked one of the babies from the protective enclosure. It bleated, and he handed it to Estelle. She took it into her arms and gave it a cuddle. "I'm going to name her Petunia. When I was small, I remember reading a book about a little lamb named Petunia. What do you think?"

"Petunia it is," Neil answered. "She'll be waiting here for you anytime you want to visit her. Remember, next year at about this time she'll have her own babies."

"I hope I get to watch them grow up too."

"You probably will." Neil smiled.

"I think I'd better get back to the school." Estelle placed the little lamb back into the enclosure with its brothers and sisters. "Thank you for giving me Petunia. I'll come to see her as often as I can. I'm glad I met you."

"Yes, me too," Neil said. "Come see me whenever you can."

Estelle sauntered back to the school building with a smile on her face. It had been the happiest day she could ever remember. Neil seemed like such a nice person. Would he think she was nice though, if he knew all about her? Probably not. She knew sooner or later she would have to tell him all the evil things she had said and done. Why had she acted in such terrible ways, causing so much trouble at Winthrop Manor? Everybody there hated her. Well, not everyone. Vera Whitaker loved her. Andy used to love her. Winnie acted like she loved her sometimes, although Estelle had grown old enough to know that the so-called "game" was some sick, perverted way for Winnie to gratify her desires. She had told her roommate about the guilty feelings she harboured, and her friend had strongly recommended that she tell Dr. Sanford about it. Estelle had not yet garnered the nerve to tell him the story.

Sometimes Vera seemed bewildered, and she had a bad memory. Estelle remembered some of the conversations they'd had—Vera often confused her.

Winnie, on the other hand, told her a lot of stories about when she was a young girl. Some of them made Estelle blush. Maybe when people got more grown-up, they made tales up about things that hadn't really happened. Estelle repeated the stories to her mother, Aunt Elisabeth, and even the vicar, only she pretended they'd been events that had happened to *her* or things *she'd* done to other people. By doing so, she found that she was able to attract a lot of attention.

She was well-aware from listening to conversations between Josephine and Aunt Elisabeth that nobody at Winthrop Manor had liked her father. He must have been a horrible person. The vicar said he was evil. He also said that about Estelle too. She didn't know whether she was evil or not. Neil didn't act like he thought she was evil. Neither did Petunia. Petunia had snuggled close to her, just as if she adored Estelle.

Maybe Vera Whitaker was evil? Maybe Winnie was too. Still, it didn't seem like they were. It was more likely that some of the things Winnie said she'd done were evil. Nevertheless, Estelle really thought they were probably lies and made-up stories. The only thing she knew for certain was that she earned a lot of attention when she did things that were supposed to be evil. Otherwise, people didn't act like they knew she was around.

16

꙳

Like turning the page in a book, Estelle matured greatly at The Sanford Institute. At first, she was hesitant to speak to Dr. Sanford in the hourly sessions set aside daily for her chat with him. It wasn't that she didn't like him. In fact, she found him very agreeable. Still, Estelle was not used to telling others about her feelings, and the person who knew her best, Winnie, always told her not to be open about conversations they had. Winnie particularly warned Estelle that she would find herself in horrendous trouble if she ever spoke about anything that had ever taken place in Vera's quarters.

However, as time passed, Estelle found it easier and easier to open up to Dr Sanford. He was the first person, outside of her family, who she had ever told that Oliver was her true father. She began to eagerly anticipate their afternoon sessions.

As she grew to know him better and truly liked him, she unburdened herself by telling all of the horrid things she'd done growing up. Things that had finally led to her living at the institute. He never became angry or made her feel ashamed. He primarily asked her questions, and for the first time in her life, she made an effort to be extremely honest. He seemed to be particularly interested in the tales she shared about the hours she'd spent playing the "game" with Winnie.

She'd finally admitted to him that many of the lies she told her mum were really events that Winnie had related about *her own* childhood. Estelle had liked Winnie so much then and thought it would be wonderful to be exactly like her when she grew up. Thus, in a strange sort of way, which she'd yet to understand, Estelle had borrowed Winnie's identity.

She wasn't at all aware that she was doing so, but her own life was so dull and boring and Winnie's sounded awfully exciting. Besides, Winnie knew a lot about so many things–particularly about what boys and girls did when they were in love. Winnie had a sister named Violet whom she hated. Estelle didn't truly hate her cousin Susan, but she was definitely envious of her, because she seemed to be so much more loved by everyone at the manor. After she overhead Josephine talking to her Aunt Elisabeth about Estelle being Oliver's daughter and not Win's, she was shocked. That had made her decide to mimic Winnie's behaviour.

After she left Dr. Sanford's office every day, she took the two hours of free time allotted to every student and wandered over to Neil Johnston's farm. He began to know exactly when she would arrive and would be waiting for her. His hair always looked like it had been freshly washed, and his clothing was spotless. It was difficult to believe that a young man could work all day on a farm, baling hay, milking cows, feeding livestock and all of the other messy chores Neil had to do, without getting dirty. After quite some time, she realised that he must have been washing up before her arrival. That made her feel very good, because *she* also made certain her hair was shiny and clean, and if necessary, changed into a different dress.

They always went to find Petunia first. Until the lamb grew too heavy, Estelle carried her. Usually she and Neil would sit down under a huge, old, oak tree, where they would talk about everything under the sun.

In the winter months, when it was too cold to sit outdoors, Neil's mother, Lillian, would serve them hot cocoa in the farmhouse kitchen. Estelle liked that old kitchen better than the fancy one at Winthrop Manor. She came to adore Mrs. Johnston, who treated her like she was special. She didn't know Mr. Johnston very well, because he was always out working on the land, but when they did finally meet, Estelle liked him a lot. She was always sorry when the time she and Neil spent together came to an end. Nevertheless, she always knew that she would see him again the next day.

She studied hard and began to excel again in her classwork. She'd forgotten how good it felt to receive A's in difficult subjects like math and science. She had always loved to read and write, so even during the time when her behavior had been abhorrent, she'd still performed well in those areas. But, to see an A on a test in chemistry or geometry made her feel marvellous.

Every semester, Dr. Sanford wrote a progress report and posted it to Josephine. Needless to say, she was utterly delighted when she learned that Estelle was performing exceptionally well at the Institute. Estelle loved the Sanford Institute so much that she begged her mum to allow her to attend summer school. Josephine was astounded and quickly gave her permission.

Dr. Sanford was no fool, and it didn't take him long to figure out that a large part of Estelle's love for the school had to do with her interest in Neil Johnston. She frequently spoke of him during their time together, and the doctor heartily approved of the relationship. He had been headmaster and psychologist at the institute from the time it opened its doors ten years previous. Thus, he was well-acquainted with a great many of the people who lived in the locale. The nearest village was Woolrich, undoubtedly because of the many sheep raised in the area. Of course, he knew the Johnstons since the school adjoined their property. They attended the same church as Dr. Sanford, and he'd met Neil when he was a young boy.

When she turned fourteen, it was hard for Estelle to accept that her school years were coming to an end. All students absolutely had to leave the Institute when they were eighteen. However, after age fourteen a student could leave if she wished. Many girls went on to study at finishing schools. She would never have believed that she would love The Sanford Institute so much that she would be sad to leave. She had, of course, returned to Winthrop Manor on holidays, and everyone had been literally astounded at the change they saw in her. At first, she could tell that Elisabeth, Tom, Susan, and even her mum were uneasy when she walked into a room. Nonetheless, they finally accepted that the change was real.

Then, everything changed beginning in the autumn of 1939. England and France declared war on Germany.

Andy was twenty-three in 1939, and had lived up to everybody's expectations. He had been an exceptional student and had grown into a stunningly handsome young man. Besides those attributes, he was exceedingly kind, thoughtful, and generous. He'd graduated Oxford and at his majority had become the new earl at Winthrop Manor. He was thankful for having spent a lot of time learning everything he could about the operation of the enormous English estate. Upon his return after commencement, Andy set about to begin running the operation side-by-side with the estate manager. Winthrop Manor was flourishing

Josephine secretly dreamed he would ride his lovely stallion, Black Star —a descendant of Black Orchid—onto the property, dismount and announce to her that he had fallen madly in love with a charming local girl. Of course, it might not turn out that way at all, but what memories it would bring if such an event did occur.

The news of the war brought fear to the entire household. Everyone directed their attention to what lay ahead. Andy stunned Josephine by announcing in the autumn of 1939, after war was declared, that he had joined the Royal Air Force and would be leaving soon for pilot training at RAF Cranwell. It was too late to beg him not to go, and it undoubtedly would have done no good anyway. Andy was just like Win. He was a patriot through and through, and nothing could have kept him from the fight. Because he was an Oxford graduate and an earl, he would automatically be placed into officer training. While Josephine was worried sick about him, she couldn't help but be proud.

Josephine accompanied him to the station when he left for his RAF training. She held him in her arms and silently prayed that he would be safe from harm. Both promised to write often, and Andy left some last-minute instructions for her to relay to the estate manager. Then, he was on the train, and Josephine could see his handsome face next to a window near the middle of the car. She threw him one last kiss and then ran back to the Rolls Royce. David drove her home while she cried every inch of the way.

More than eight months after Andy's entrance into the RAF, he was ready to put his pilot skills to use. After basic training was accomplished at the end of April 1940, Andy had completed seven months of flight training. He had completed three types of training. The first was Elementary Flying Training School using aircraft such as the Tiger Moth. The second stage of training was Service Flight Training, which included Initial and Advanced Training. During that period, Advanced Trainers such as the Master were introduced. The third and final phase introduced the trainee to front line aircraft and trained them how to fly and fight.

During the early stage of the war, the aircraft had difficulties. In the first few months of 1940 there were few Hurricanes to spare and almost no Spitfires, Britain's newest and most highly regarded fighter. As a result, fighter pilots often had to spend some of this time flying biplanes and bomber trainees in battles.

Fortunately for Andy, 'round May 1940 that situation eased and Hurricanes were more common in the OTU. The lack of modern fighters in the first few months of 1940 sent some pilots to squadrons with a limited number of hours on Spitfires and Hurricanes. Nevertheless, newly minted RAF pilots like 2nd Lieutenant Andrew Winthrop were ready and eager to put their skills into practice, along with their dreams to pilot a Spitfire.

There had been total inactivity between the Allied and Axis troops since the declaration of war in September of 1939. In fact, so little had occurred that the Brits had begun to call the state of affairs the "phony war." However, military mothers like Josephine were concerned about the prevailing quiet. All were praying that there really wouldn't be war and that the young soldiers would be home by Christmas. That didn't happen, however, and soldiers were being prepared by the thousands to eventually face the enemy.

The early stages of World War II saw successful German invasions on the continent aided decisively by the air power of the Luftwaffe, which was able to establish tactical air superiority with great efficiency. The speed with which German forces defeated most of the defending armies in Norway in early 1940, created a significant political crisis in Britain. On May 10, the same day Winston Churchill became British Prime Minister, the Germans started the Battle of France with a massive penetration of French territory.

This is what Andy had been waiting for. RAF Fighter Command was urgently short of trained pilots and aircraft, but despite the protests of its commander, Hugh Dowding, who believed forces would leave home defences under-strength, Winston Churchill sent fighter squadrons anyway. They were the Air Component of the British Expeditionary Force, and their mission was to support operations in France. By May 26, 1940, the Germans had literally cornered British, Belgian, and French Resistance troops at the port of Dunkirk, isolating them on the beaches. Completely surrounded, the Royal Navy put into motion Operation Dynamo to rescue soldiers who were easy targets for German dive bombers and Bf 109 fighter units.

Dunkirk was beginning to look like a monumental tragedy. Nonetheless, it became a successful tale of evacuation, due not only to the RAF and the fifteen Spitfire squadrons sent into battle, but to the citizens of Great Britain, young and old—in and out of uniform. The War Office decided to evacuate British forces from France on May 25, 1940. During the following nine days, more than three hundred thousand men escaped aboard 861 vessels (of which 243 were sunk during the operation).

Andy's aviation skills were badly needed as the RAF was assigned the task of providing cover for the troops congregated on the French beaches at Dunkirk waiting to be transported to English soil. Many hundreds lost their lives as they were strafed by the Luftwaffe while standing unprotected, praying to be rescued by a ship or boat.

It was a nightmare, but also a miraculous example of courage as men from across the British Isles made their way across the English Channel in watercraft of every imaginable sort, from naval vessels of enormous size to small pleasure craft and fishing boats. Upon arrival, they were sent to the French beaches of the channel to rescue men who stood waist-deep in water while German Luftwaffe and British RAF aeroplanes became embroiled in dogfights above the helpless men. Thousands of soldiers, including members of the French Resistance Fighters, were rescued during the dangerous operation. The citizens of England now had no doubt that they were at war.

Andy was one of the RAF pilots who battled the Luftwaffe above the beaches of Dunkirk. Mercifully, he survived the horrendous battle and had a hand in saving a multitude of Allied lives. When it was over, he was granted a two-week leave from his unit. Naturally, he bolted for Winthrop Manor. Shortly after the dreadful event which became known as The Dunkirk Miracle, since so many British citizens had helped to save so many of their countrymen, the Germans invaded France and the country fell to the Axis countries. The people of England were overcome with grief when the Nazi flag began to fly over the Place de la Concorde. It was June 19, 1940.

Next came the Battle of Britain, but there was a brief respite before the Luftwaffe sent their deplorable aeroplanes to Britain in an attempt to destroy the capital city and airfields.

❧❧

In September of 1941, upon returning to school, Estelle made her usual visit to Neil's farmhouse. It was clear to everyone who knew them that strong feelings had developed between them, although both were still quite young. As the school year progressed and news of the dreadful war became more and more dismal, many things changed. Rationing of petrol and food was put into effect and many of Estelle's friends had boyfriends who enlisted in the military. The Americans had joined the battle when Japan bombed their naval base at Pearl Harbor in the Hawaiian Islands in December. She worried continually about Andy.

When February arrived, she turned sixteen. In May, she made her daily visit to Neil. Before she could even reach the barn, she saw him come running down the hill at an astonishing speed. She could see his mother standing by the front doorway, holding a handkerchief and dabbing at her eyes, weeping. When he reached Estelle, he was out of breath and appeared to be very excited. "Goodness," she cried. "Whatever has you in such a kerfuffle?"

"Oh, Estelle. You won't believe my news. It's so exciting. I don't think I've mentioned that today is my nineteenth birthday!"

"No. I didn't know that. Happy Birthday, Neil. You remember I was sixteen in February?"

"Of course, I do," he answered. "You always wear the bracelet I gave you for your birthday."

"Yes, I do," she said, with a smile. "If I'd known it was your birthday I would have given you a gift."

"That doesn't matter. I didn't expect a gift from you. Well, maybe I will, someday." His voice was teasing. She didn't know what he meant.

"Guess what? I've enlisted in the First Battalion, East Surrey Regiment, and will be training at Chatham Barracks in Kent. I report for my medical examination on October second."

"But, Neil, you wouldn't have had to join up. Why are you going now? You could have been exempted because you are an only son and your occupation is farming."

"Estelle. It's every Englishman's duty. I want to go. I want to fight for my country. You've always sounded so proud of your brother, Andy. Aren't you proud of me?"

"Well, yes, but Andy is an officer—a pilot in the RAF. That's different. He's also older. Why do you want to take the chance of being shot? He's been through some horrendous battles."

"No, Estelle. I would never have done that. Of course, I don't want to be shot. However, that's the chance a soldier has to take. I'll be well-trained. Anyway, we cannot let the Huns beat us. My God, Estelle, look what happened at Dunkirk, the Battle of Britain, the Blitz, and all of it. I considered joining up when I was eighteen, but my parents convinced me to wait a year. Then, they said if the war was still going on, I could go."

With no warning, Estelle began to weep. Tears streamed down her cheeks, she gulped sobs, and was breathless. "Oh, Neil. I'm frightened for you. I've grown to know you so well. Of course, I do understand. I know you aren't a coward. Still, what if something happens to you? You could be sent anywhere. You might be killed. Oh, God, I don't think I could bear that."

"Estelle, I promise I'll take good care. I'm not terribly keen on being killed either." He smiled. "I hope you'll write to me. They say nothing is more important than letters to a soldier."

"Of course, I'll write to you. I'll have to give you my address at Winthrop Manor. I'll be leaving school in May."

"Are you going away to another school, then?" Neil asked.

"No. I don't think so. I might have, but now with the war, I think I'll stay at Winthrop Manor. I want to spend time with my family and learn to know them now that I understand myself so much better."

"Perhaps you'd like to take Petunia home with you. She might make you feel less lonely and remind you of me."

"Oh, Neil. Could I? Would your parents mind?" She had extracted a white linen handkerchief from her pocket and wiped her tears.

"No. I'm sure they would think it's fine. They both like you a lot. Mum says it's sweet that you're so attached to Petunia."

"I dearly love her, Neil. I think she may be the only living creature that has ever really loved me too."

"That isn't true," he answered. "Not at all. Would you think me very forward if I told you that I believe I love you?"

"Neil. Are you serious? How can you say that when you don't really know everything about me?" Estelle was thrilled at his words, but she also felt that he would change his mind if she told him everything about her past. After all, he was now nineteen years old, and she was only sixteen. Was she too young to be thinking of love?

"I'm serious, Estelle. I feel I know you awfully well. This isn't the first time you've hinted that there are things I don't know about you. You once told me that someday you would share those secrets with me. I can't think of anything that would change my feelings about you. Could you take the time to tell me now?"

Estelle stood quietly, looking at the ground. She was afraid. The fact that Neil had told her he loved her made her feel a warm glow all over. What if she was to tell him about the many evil things she had said and done in the past? Would he decide that he never wanted to see her again?

After a few moments of silence, she made the decision to be honest with him. Either she did so now or she might never have another chance. He took her hand, and led her to their large oak tree. Taking off his jacket, he spread it on the ground and motioned for Estelle to sit down next to him. "All right. Please tell what sins you believe you've committed."

"It's a very long story," she began.

It took over an hour for her to tell him everything. She was particularly embarrassed when she told him about the stories she'd concocted regarding nasty things she'd supposedly done with the vicar.

"Did you honestly do that stuff?" he asked.

"No. I lied. Someone I know told me she'd had that sort of experience with a Catholic priest. I knew if I told my mother that I'd done it, she would be fiercely irritated. I've been filled with anger most of my life. I overheard my mum talking to my aunt, telling her that my real father was my uncle, Oliver; he was Mum's husband's brother. She told me that Oliver raped her, and that's how she had me, but I don't know if that's true or not. They might have had an affair."

"Do you really think she'd say something so bad about her husband's brother if it wasn't true?"

"I don't know. She really hated Oliver. I don't think he was a very nice person. He tried to kidnap my brother Andy when he was a baby. Oliver was going to have him adopted out. Oliver thought his brother, Win, wasn't going to come home from the Great War. Win had been missing for a long time. If Andy was out of the picture, that would have meant Oliver would be the next Earl of Winthrop."

Neil put his arm around Estelle's shoulder. "You've had a bad patch of it. I think you are too hard on yourself."

"You don't think I'm an awful person?"

He reached over and put both arms 'round her. "No. I think I love you even more because you haven't had an easy life. Come here." He pulled her close to him. "Have you ever been kissed? I mean, kissed for real?"

"Not by anybody other than my brother, and a few times my mum has kissed me. The retired cook at our house, Vera, has kissed me too."

"Well, what about trying an honest-to-goodness kiss?"

"All right. I think I'd like that a lot."

Neil held her even more tightly and put his lips upon hers. She wrapped her arms 'round him. The kiss intensified. He ran his hands through her hair, and she placed hers on the back of his head. His blond strands felt silky. Pulling away from her for only a moment, he whispered, "I love you dearly, Estelle. More dearly than words can ever tell."

"Oh, Neil. I love you too," she murmured. "I've felt this way a long time, but I didn't think there would be any chance you would feel the same way. Now, here you are going away to the war. I shall miss you so much."

"I'll be back, I promise. Now that I have you to come back to it will make me be even more careful."

They kissed again and again. Estelle wondered if he was going to do any of the things she knew some boys did to girls. But he didn't. "I love you too much to let this go any further," he softly said. "When that day comes, it will be perfect. You're awfully young right now. We'll be married when you're older. Would you like that?"

"Do you mean we would be engaged while you're off fighting? Oh, Neil, do you honestly mean that?"

"Yes, I do. But, again, Estelle, you're young. If you change your mind or meet someone else while I'm gone, I'll understand. I've never meant anything more in my life. I wish I had a ring to give you. I'll buy one when I get my first leave. I want to know you have it on your hand while I'm gone."

"Oh Neil. I'm not too young. Really, I'm not. However, I'll wait until you think I'm the proper age. Please, though, don't make me wait until I'm twenty-one. I've never been so happy in my life. I didn't think I'd ever get married. Or that anyone would love me so much. I'll do everything in the world to be the best wife in the world. I must take you to Winthrop Manor before you leave. My mum won't believe this. I know she'll like you though. Who wouldn't?" Estelle grinned.

A bell rang in the distance. "Oh my," said Estelle. "That's the dinner bell. How long have we been here? I hope I'm not in trouble."

Neil stood and pulled Estelle to her feet. "Come, my sweet girl. I'll walk back to the school with you. They'd better not be mad at you. I'll tell them I love you, and that we're going to be married. I'll also tell them I'm about to be a soldier. Surely they can't begrudge a fellow a bit of time with his sweetheart before he goes off to war."

Estelle lay sleepless that night, going over and over in her mind every word Neil had spoken to her. She would soon have a ring to prove she was an engaged lady. It was so hard to believe. The next dilemma she faced was telling her mum that she wanted to bring Neil home to meet the family. She didn't plan to tell Josephine about the engagement until after a visit to Winthrop Manor had taken place. She had mentioned Neil in the weekly letters she wrote home and had also recited the tale about his having given her Petunia. Of course, all those things had taken place before his announcement about joining the military. Now, it would be necessary to announce that Petunia would be joining the other animals at the manor. Estelle wasn't very worried about that declaration, since animals were plentiful at their spacious estate, and her mum had always loved pets of every sort, although dogs, cats, and horses were the most beloved creatures. Still, sheep were raised at the manor, so Petunia would beyond any doubt fit in splendidly.

More important than the Petunia problem was the proclamation that she and Neil were engaged to be married. Estelle had no idea how her mum would react to such news. She was glad she'd been honest with Neil about the difficulties she'd caused while growing up at Winthrop Manor. She had matured immensely since her stay at the Sanford Institute, and she wanted desperately for her mother to recognise the changes that had occurred since leaving home. Though she knew her mum had definitely seen the difference when Estelle had visited on holidays, there were still things she wanted Mum to know. While Estelle wasn't at all certain it was the school that had begun her journey of growth, she emphatically knew that she was scarcely the same wretched girl who had left Winthrop Manor in the autumn of 1933. Had it been nine years? She was such a completely different person.

A week after Neil proposed to her, he presented her with an amethyst set in gold and surrounded by small diamonds. He knew her birthday was in February and that her birthstone was an amethyst. She was so thrilled and vowed to never, ever take it off. When she returned to her room at the school, she was changing into her dress for the afternoon meal when there was a knock on her door. Opening it, she saw Dr. Sanford. He had never before visited her room.

"Good evening, Estelle," he began. "I'm sorry to disturb you, but you have a long-distance telephone call in my office. Could you come immediately?"

"A long-distance telephone call for me?" she echoed. "Who in the world would be calling me here?"

"I believe it's your mother. Come with me now and then you can return to your room to finish dressing for lunch."

Estelle put on her shoes, as she was still in her stocking feet, and followed him down the corridor leading to his office. Upon entering it, she saw that the telephone on his desk had the receiver out of its cradle. She walked quickly to the desk and picked it up. "Hello, this is Estelle."

"Estelle, it's Mummy. Something sad has happened. My Uncle Roderick has passed away. I'd like you to be here for the funeral service."

"Oh, Mum, I am sorry. I loved him. He was a dear man. What happened?"

"He had a heart seizure. It was very quick, and Dr. Tom said it was painless. He was very old, you know. I suppose we should have expected something of the sort."

"Shall I grab a train to Winthrop-on-Hart?" Estelle asked.

"No. Andy is being given compassionate leave, so he will be driving home in a borrowed auto. He said he'll pick you up at the school later today."

"Oh, all right. Shall I pack all black clothing?" Estelle enquired.

"Yes. That would be suitable. The service will be tomorrow, and if you'd like, you may stay here a few extra days."

"Yes, I'd like that." Her heart was beating quickly. Suddenly she'd realised that the trip to Winthrop Manor would be a perfect time to bring Neil to meet her family. However, did she have the courage to ask her mother? It was a somewhat odd time to be bringing her fiancé home. Would Mummy object?

Estelle took a deep breath. "Mummy, I'd like to ask your permission to bring someone very special with me. I know I've mentioned Neil Johnston to you before, and now, well, we've become engaged. He gave me a smashing ring. Of course, we don't intend to marry until he comes back from the war. He's joined the military and will be leaving for Salisbury Plain for artillery training in just five weeks now. I understand that this is a bad time to introduce him to everybody, but if I don't do so now, he'll be gone and I don't know how long it will be before I can do so. Oh, do say yes, Mummy."

Josephine was startled. Estelle sounded so different. She very seldom, if ever, called her "Mummy," but she also sounded happy – immensely happy. And sweet. Yes, sweet. It was a word she would never have associated with Estelle. It didn't seem at all an appropriate time to meet a daughter's fiancé, yet Josephine couldn't find it in her heart to say no to this young lady who had always before been such a challenge.

"It would be unusual. Nevertheless, considering the war and his having to leave for training, perhaps we can make an exception. Yes. All right, Estelle. Bring him with you. Of course, I want very much to meet him. I'll inform Andy about the change in plans. I'm certain he'll be pleased to have Neil accompany both of you on your journey home."

"Oh, Mummy. Thank you so much. You'll like him, I promise. I love him so."

"I'm happy for you, Estelle. Do tell him that the family is eager to meet him. I'll look forward to seeing you this evening. Now, please put Dr. Sanford back on the line so I may tell him the arrangements. You'll need permission to leave the campus."

Estelle handed the telephone back to Dr. Sanford and quickly left his office. She was afraid she was about to burst into tears. Happiness was not an emotion Estelle was very familiar with. Yet, she was absolutely filled with joy. On the walk back to her room, she realised that she needed to tell Neil of the arrangements she'd just made. Stopping in the middle of the corridor, she turned and hurriedly walked back to Dr. Sanford's office. He was sitting at his desk writing something.

"Dr. Sanford, excuse me for disturbing you. As you know already, I'm to be leaving here to journey home for a funeral. My mum has given permission for me to bring my fiancé with me," she nervously said.

"Yes, Estelle. Your mother said as much. I had no idea you were engaged. Who is the young man, and when did this occur?"

"Dr. Sanford, I know I've mentioned Neil Johnston to you before. You remember, don't you?" She was trembling. Was she in trouble?

He smiled. "Yes, of course I remember. I'm only surprised this happened and you apparently didn't feel you could tell me."

Estelle reached her hand out, showing him the engagement ring. "He told me he loved me last week. I did mean to share the news with you, but I was so undone. Then, he gave me this ring. It's my birthstone. Isn't it grand?"

"Indeed, it is," he replied. "I do hope you aren't planning on marriage too quickly. You've made wonderful progress here at the Institute. Still, I'd like to see you sort yourself out a bit more before becoming a wife."

"Oh, no. We won't even think of marriage until this wretched war is over. Neil has joined up and will be leaving for training in five weeks. You have helped me so much. I want to continue to grow and learn more about myself and come to know my family better, so I'll be leaving here in February," Estelle replied emphatically. "The reason I came back to your office is that I need to go over to Neil's farm and inform him of the plans for us to travel to Winthrop Manor this afternoon when my brother Andy arrives to pick us up. Do I have your consent to do so?"

"Certainly," he responded. "You may also absent yourself from lunch, if need be. I know you must pack and ready yourself for the journey."

"Thank you so much, sir. I'm leaving right now for Neil's farm. You're right. I probably won't be able to be present for lunch. My brother will undoubtedly stop at a pub for a quick bite on the way to my home."

"That will be fine, Estelle," Dr. Sanford replied.

Estelle turned and scurried toward the doorway.

"Oh, and Estelle," the doctor exclaimed. "Best wishes on your engagement. I'm most happy for you."

At a little after eight o'clock that evening, Andy, Estelle, and Neil arrived at Winthrop Manor. The ride from The Sanford Institute had been enjoyable for everybody. At first, Neil was rather quiet, but as he warmed to Andy, they began to chat about all things military and Estelle quietly listened to their conversation. She was happy that they seemed to like each other. By the time they were close to Winthrop-on-Hart, she had no worries about whether Andy approved of the engagement. He had said so himself. Just before they made the turn into the gravelled drive leading to the estate, Andy turned to Estelle and said that he thought she had picked a fiancé from the top of the barrel. She grinned, and reached over to hold Neil's hand.

Upon entering the manor, Josephine was at the door to greet them. Estelle gave her a giant hug and again called her Mummy. She then turned and introduced Neil, who said, "How nice to make your acquaintance, Lady Josephine."

At the same time, Estelle was showing her mother the engagement ring. "Isn't it beautiful?" she asked.

Josephine took her daughter's hand and marveled at the amethyst. One would have thought that Estelle was wearing one of the crown jewels. She wondered if Neil could be feeling awkward., coming from a much different household. He had never seen, let alone been,in a home like Winthrop Manor. She suspected he was making every effort not to show astonishment at his surroundings. However, he must have known that he was welcome.

"Now Neil," said Josephine, "I want you to feel comfortable here. You needn't refer to me as Lady Josephine. I'm Estelle's mother. Since the two of you are engaged to be married, please feel free to be less formal."

"Oh ma'am, I don't believe it would be proper not to use your title. My parents raised me correctly."

"I'm sure they did, Neil, but I would honestly feel uneasy if you treated me as you would a stranger who happens to have a title. Do you think you might be able to call me Miss Josephine or perhaps Mrs. Winthrop?"

"Yes, ma'am, I could try, Mrs. Winthrop."

"All right. That will do for now. After you and Estelle are married, I hope you will feel comfortable either using my given name only, or of course, mum, if you wish."

"Once we're married, perhaps I'll feel differently," he replied.

"Let's go into the drawing room," Josephine said. "We can be more comfortable. We need to have a nice, long chat. I want to know everything about the handsome man my daughter has chosen to marry."

Neil blushed when she referred to him as handsome, although he truly was.

Andy spoke up. "Mum, you're embarrassing Neil. I've had a chance to become well-acquainted with him during our journey. He's a good chap. I look forward to being his brother-in-law."

The four made their way to the opulent drawing room where Estelle and Neil sat next to one another on the white sofa in front of the fireplace and Andy and Josephine were opposite them in two winged-back chairs.

"My goodness, this brings back memories from long ago," Josephine said. "I can recall like it was yesterday when Win brought me here for the first time. We sat in this very room, and I was so frightened. His mother, Lady Beatrice, scared the devil out of me. You see, Neil, I was a simple girl, and Mother Winthrop was not at all happy that Win had chosen me to be his wife. I ended up in tears. So, you see, you needn't be concerned that I'm a highbrow aristocrat. I know exactly how it feels to be looked down upon by a person of the gentry. I don't ever want you to experience those feelings."

"No, Mrs. Winthrop. You've made me feel very welcome. I may not be an aristocrat, but I promise that I love Estelle with all my heart, and I'll always take the best care of her." He glanced at Estelle with an adoring look. It was obvious that they were deeply in love.

Josephine had to hold back tears because the situation was so reminiscent of the way she and Win had felt.

Neil looked at her with sorrow. "Mrs. Winthrop, I'm dreadfully sorry that you've lost your uncle. Estelle has told me that he was a very fine man. I wish I could have known him. Please do accept my condolences."

"How thoughtful and kind of you, Neil," Josephine responded. "Yes, he was indeed a fine man. Did Estelle tell you that he literally raised me from the time my parents died when the *Titanic* went down?"

"Yes. What a dreadful tragedy that was. You must have felt fortunate to have had someone you loved as much as you did your uncle. Estelle has told me that he was like a father to you."

"He absolutely was. There were many times that I don't know what I would have done without him. I'm grateful that he lived such a long life with no ill health and all of his facilities until the very end. I shall miss him greatly."

"I want to thank you for allowing me to pay a visit to your home at such a wretched time."

"Oh, Neil, I rather think your being here will help to ease the pain. As the saying goes, 'One door closes and another opens.' Your presence and the news of your engagement have brought happiness. I believe Uncle Roderick would have wanted it to be that way," Josephine said.

Andy changed the subject. "Mum, did we arrive too late for dinner? To be honest, we only had a bit to eat at a small pub on the way here. I don't know about Estelle and Neil, but I'm starving."

"Darling, I'm so sorry. I should have told you that I had Mrs. Boyle hold dinner until you arrived. Why don't I show Neil to his room, and you can freshen up before we dine. Don't be concerned about formality. Come, follow me." Josephine rose from her chair.

⁋٨∝

The next few days flew by. Between the funeral service for Roderick and a reception following at Winthrop Manor, as well as a hastily put together engagement party for Estelle and Neil, there was scarcely any time for simple relaxation. Nonetheless, even with the sorrow accompanying Roderick's death, Winthrop Manor hadn't been filled with so much joy in a long time. Everyone from Tom and Elisabeth to their daughter Susan, as well as the entire staff, adored Neil. They were all amazed at the apparent change in Estelle's behaviour. She literally glowed with happiness and was loving and kind to everyone.

Vera was thrilled to see her, and Winnie acted as if a long-lost friend had returned. In a certain way that was true. Estelle had spent untold hours chatting with Vera, and Winnie had usually been present.

Josephine was a bit puzzled at Estelle's reaction when Winnie hugged and welcomed Estelle home. Her daughter was so delighted to see all the family and the staff at Winthrop Manor, but she was aloof with Winnie.

She would never have believed that she would be sorry to see Estelle leave, but indeed she was. Estelle had now become the daughter she'd always longed for. Whether the change was due to The Sanford Institute or her love for Neil, there was no question that it was certainly real. Josephine was eager for a suitable time when she could sit down with Estelle and talk at length about the clearly remarkable changes in her personality.

17

❦

The visit to Winthrop Manor ended all too quickly. In what seemed the blink of an eye, Estelle found herself at the railway station near her school with Neil's arms wrapped tightly about her as she wept and held him equally tight. His parents had said their goodbyes at the farm, as he had requested, since he wanted to spend his last moments as a civilian alone with his fiancée.

When the conductor called for all to board the train headed for Chatham in Kent, the lovers passionately kissed and repeated promises to write letters. Then before Estelle could say all the things she'd rehearsed, Neil was already in the railroad coach leaving the station.

It was October 9, 1942. Britain had maintained control of the skies, but an unimaginable amount of damage had been done to London. The East End in particular had nearly been destroyed, and even Buckingham Palace had been damaged due to German bombs. Still, the RAF had demonstrated its skill, and Winston Churchill made a speech about the heroism of the Royal Air Force, in which he proclaimed, "Never had so many owed so much to so few."

❦

Before reporting for training, Neil had been medically examined and given The King's Shilling together with a regimental number. Then he was told to take seven days leave before reporting for service. Those days had been heavenly. He and Estelle had spent every possible moment together. After his leave, he had been instructed to report to Chatham Barracks in Kent.

When he reported to the guard room still wearing civilian clothes, the sentries posted at the entrance reminded him of the tiny toy soldiers Neil's parents had given him for gifts as a boy.

Estelle received his first letter nearly two weeks after she had kissed him goodbye. She had written every day, but hadn't expected that he would be able to do so, as he was already aware that the period of training would be rough. When that first letter arrived, Estelle ran to the spot where Neil had proposed to her, near the old oak tree, and sat beneath it to read every word several times.

Dearest Estelle,

As new recruits, we are known as rookies. After a few days at the barracks and after doing a little training in our civilian clothes, we were all issued our uniform and gas masks. We then received an identity disc with our number on i, together with the most important item of kit – our rifle. We were told this may mean being killed or saved, as this will be our first line of defence against the enemy.

The army training at Chatham is coming a little easier for me thanks to my farm life, lifting bales of hay, and working long, hard days. I discovered the march and position of arms are different, as is the salute. However, in time everything seems to go according to plan. The Royal Navy is not far from us and for our gas training we have to share the gas chambers with them. The chambers are not very pleasant as they contained mustard gas and tear gas, but it is necessary for us to experience them and know the affects and treatment for them.

At the time while all this is going on, we need to be aware that an air raid is always possible, so we listen for the air raid warning to tell us the enemy planes are on their way. We have to be on our guard all the time, our gas masks and tin helmets ready for the warning. The lenses of our gas masks have to be cleaned quite often with anti-gas ointment, to ensure we'd be able to see clearly because they easily mist over with our breath.

I miss you so very much. Every night before I go to sleep, I say a prayer that God will see us both through this miserable war. I long for the day when I can hold you in my arms and kiss your beautiful lips. I believe I'll be granted leave after the four-month training is completed, but that seems like an awfully long time. That will be around the middle of February, I guess.

I promise to write again very soon, and remember, I love you. Take good care of Petunia.
Neil

Estelle re-read the letter several times, especially the romantic sections. When she returned to her room, she circled the month of February on the calendar. Not only would Neil be returning sometime during that month, but she would turn nineteen on February twenty-third. The next letter she received didn't arrive until late November. It was once again filled with military news, but there was also a sentence which sent her heart soaring.

Dearest Estelle,

I'm so sorry it has been such a long time since I've written. During my stay at Chatham there have been many unpleasant incidents. Worst of all was when a section of us left the barracks to march down the road one dark night to have a bath. As we marched along, a heavy vehicle went into the back of the section, killing many in the incident. A neon back lamp, showing a red or green light, wasn't being carried. From then on, whenever marches go to have a bath in the evening, we are detailed to have a lamp at the back of the section as well as the front. Don't be alarmed. I'm fine.

I received your letter about your birthday. Of course, I knew that date but hadn't made the connection between completion of my training and you turning seventeen. I am going to try to determine exactly when I'll be given leave before I'm given my first assignment. If it is at all possible, I would like for us to be married on your birthday. Seventeen is old enough to be married. I'm willing to wait, of course. I do know a lot of chaps here with me who have wives who are even younger than seventeen. I guess the war has changed many things. If not on that exact date, then do you think we could pick a date when I'm home during that month? I know we decided we would wait until the war has ended, but I know a lot more now than I did then, and it is very possible that this is going to be a very long siege. I'd like to know that you are my wife before I leave again.

Please let me know your thoughts. I love you so.
Neil

Estelle was ecstatic. She ran into the school, and asked Dr. Sanford if she might use the telephone to call her mother. He enquired as to why she needed to make such a call, and she explained about Neil's letter. She was somewhat ill at ease, since she remembered that he had told her not to marry too quickly. However, he smiled and said he thought Estelle and Neil had waited long enough. He understood that the war might go on for a substantial length of time and many young people were making the decision to marry before soldiers were sent to far-away places for God only knew how long. Naturally, he gave his permission for use of the telephone.

Estelle placed a call to Winthrop Manor and Radcliffe answered on the first ring. Estelle asked to speak to her mother. She noticed her hands were shaking. Thank goodness Josephine was there. In short order, she came on the line.

"Estelle? Radcliffe said it was you. Is everything all right?" During the difficult time of war, Josephine's words were most often the first spoken by anyone receiving a long-distance telephone call.

"Yes, Mummy, I'm fine. Neil is fine. In fact, everything is splendid. I've just had a letter from him. Oh, Mummy, he wants us to be married when he completes his training at Chatham. I'm just ecstatic. He doesn't know the precise date yet, but it will be sometime in February. We don't want a large, fancy wedding, just a small ceremony in the chapel at Winthrop Manor, so there wouldn't be a lot of tasks for you. I would hand-write some nice invitations. I wouldn't need a fancy gown. I'd probably only have Susan as an attendant. I don't know who Neil would choose to stand up for him. Perhaps Andy, if he could obtain leave from the RAF. Other than those simple plans, of course I'd like flowers and perhaps we could do a reception at Winthrop Manor. We would only invite friends and family. I'll be seventeen by then. Oh, please, please say yes, Mummy."

Josephine's memory immediately went back to 1914 when she and Win eloped to Scotland on the eve of the Great War. She knew what it was like to be over-the-top in love. She also knew that the only reason they had eloped was because Win's parents were so adamant that they shouldn't marry. Josephine had no intention of repeating Lady Beatrice and Lord Rupert's behaviour. She would make certain that her daughter was wed exactly where she should be—at her own home in the ancient chapel where countless generations of brides had taken their vows. "Of course, I give my permission. Everybody here adores Neil. I understand what it's like to love someone who is going to war. However, darling, you will have a gown. I'd like for you to wear mine. It belonged to my mother. When Win and I eloped to Gretna Green with Elisabeth and Andrew, I wore it."

"Oh, my goodness. I never dreamed of anything so remarkable. You mean you'd be willing to lend it to me?" Estelle cried in amazement.

"I wouldn't be lending it to you. I'd be passing it down to you, with the hope that someday you'll have your own daughter and the tradition would continue."

"What a beautiful thought," Estelle replied. "Mummy, thank you so much for being so forgiving to me. I was such a horrible child, really a terrible person. I'm so sorry I did such wretched things to cause so much heartache I intend to spend the rest of my life trying to make up for the malicious, malevolent times when I caused you so much pain. Sending me here to the Sanford Institute was the best thing you ever might have done. I understand myself now."

"We all noticed such a change in you when you visited during Uncle Roderick's funeral. No one could believe you were the same person. What brought about such a remarkable difference?" Josephine asked.

"Oh, Mummy. There are a lot of things I never told you. I truly despise bringing harm to anyone, but I do think it's time I tell you. I probably should have long ago, but I was awfully confused." Estelle sat down in a chair beside Dr. Sanford's desk. He had left his office to allow her privacy. Tears began to well in her eyes.

"Whatever do you mean, Estelle? What are the things you never told me? Please be honest now. If there is something I should know, then tell me," Josephine said, in a pleading voice.

Estelle sat still for just a moment. It was hard to put together the correct words to make her mother understand everything. "Well, Mummy," she began. "I guess it all started when I found out that Oliver was my real father. I was horrified. Of course, I was very young, but it hurt awfully bad. Everyone had always said he was such a terrible person. Then, the worst possible thing that could have happened took place. Winnie came to be Vera's companion. Well, not exactly when she came, but when she began to have a profound influence upon me." Estelle was clearly weeping now, as memories flooded her mind. "You see, when I was about four, she began to do some truly wicked things to me. Do you recall how I used to spend hours in Vera's quarters?"

"Yes, of course," replied Josephine. "I thought it was quite sweet that you seemed to like Vera so much. I knew it meant a lot to her to have you as company."

"Yes, I suppose it did. Nonetheless, Vera would often doze off when I was in her room. When that happened, I would tell Winnie I was going to go to my own room. But Winnie would tell me to stay, and she would tell stories about when she was growing up. She also said she would teach me things. Of course, I was just a small girl, and I loved to hear stories about people's lives and was curious about what she would teach me."

"Yes, I'm curious too." Josephine's voice held a note of apprehension.

"For a long time she told me tales about what an evil little girl she'd been. Most of the lies I told you and others came straight out of Winnie's mouth. She told me she'd had a sinful relationship with a Catholic priest. That's how I invented the lie about Father Comer and me. There were many other tales like that. She also told me that she'd put out her brother's eye by throwing scissors at him. So, guess where I got the idea to do the same thing to Susan? I don't know if the stories she told me were true, but I thought they were. Then, she started to do stuff to me."

"What sort of stuff?" Josephine asked, with enormous apprehension.

"Um… Mummy, it's sort-of embarrassing to tell you these things. But, Dr. Sanford says I shouldn't be embarrassed, and that I'm not the one who did anything wrong. Still, for a long time, I thought I was very evil."

"Oh my God, Estelle. Your family, including me, didn't help at all. We added to such feelings by saying you were evil and immoral." Josephine was mortified.

"That wasn't your fault, Mummy. I did act atrociously."

"Anyway, please tell me, Estelle. What did Winnie do to you?"

"Well… she started by telling me we were going to play a game, having me get undressed and then she would put her fingers inside of me. You know what I mean. She would ask me if it felt good. It didn't, but I lied." By then, Estelle was openly sobbing. "Once, she hung me upside down in the closet. That's where I got the idea to hang Susan in the dirty laundry space."

"Oh my God! Estelle, I am so sorry. How could I not have figured out that something like that was happening? It never crossed my mind."

"I don't think it would have crossed anyone's mind. Winnie can act so sweet. Anyway, that's where most of my bad behaviour came from. Sometimes, Winnie would lay on top of me. When it was all over, she would present me with a lovely gift. Do you remember the pretty dolls I was given and the doll house? Oh, there were so many things."

"Yes, yes. I thought Vera and Winnie were just spoiling you a bit," answered Josephine.

"I also told her about Oliver being my father. She told me you'd had an affaire with him and were a shameful, disgusting trollop. Of course, I believed her, and it made me hate you. She played with my mind with all sorts of lies. Dr. Sanford says she's mentally disturbed," Estelle cried.

"What a truly vile human being. Oh, Estelle, I must let Winnie go immediately. Thank goodness we've not had any other small children in the house. She never did anything like these things to Susan did she? At least that you know about?"

"No, I'm almost certain she didn't. It was probably the best thing ever that Tom, Elisabeth, and Susan moved back to Cloverdale.".

"Do you think she could be doing awful things to Vera? After all, Vera's mind has been deteriorating for a long while."

"No, Mummy, I don't think that would have ever happened. Winnie told me she rather prefers young girls."

Josephine was beside herself. As she spoke on the telephone, she ran her hands through her hair and bit her nails. She, too, was weeping. "Estelle. I must ring off. I need to confront Winnie immediately. I am truly delighted about your wedding plans, and thank you so much for telling me everything about Winnie. I'm absolutely heartbroken that I allowed such a person to live under the Winthrop Manor roof, but most of all that she perpetrated such horrendous, immoral acts right under my nose. I'm so dreadfully sorry, Estelle. I should have recognised that a child who was so decent and kind could have modified her behaviour so greatly, without some underlying cause. I was so horribly wrong, Estelle. I do pray you'll be able to forgive me."

"There is nothing to forgive. You couldn't have known. I'm glad you're going to confront Winnie. After you've dealt with her, could you please send me your wedding gown so I can see if it will need to be altered?" Estelle asked.

"Darling, you'll be home for Christmas very soon. You can try it on then and we'll see what, if anything, needs to be done. I love you, sweetheart. Thank you again for telling me everything. I'll ring you later to tell you how my conversation with Winnie goes."

✌✙✙

Without delay, Josephine notified the authorities, who immediately took Winnie into custody. Winnie admitted to her ghastly behavior, so there was no need for any lengthy-legal action. Besides validating the information Estelle had provided, Josephine also rang the persons who were given as references when she had been hired to be Vera's companion. None of the people existed. Josephine learned a valuable lesson from the entire episode.

As soon as all this had been accomplished, she rang Estelle and told her that Winnie had been dismissed and was no longer at Winthrop Manor.

Josephine called the entire family and staff together, as well as the now-married Hope and Vicar Howe and shared the story with them. Her aim was to make certain that any remaining negative feelings toward Estelle were eliminated. When everybody heard what the poor girl had endured, they were infuriated with Winnie as well as horrified at what Estelle had experienced. They also felt guilty because they had never considered the possibility that something evil had happened to Estelle. Hope offered to take over duties of companion to Vera, since she dearly loved the elderly woman. That turned out to be a true blessing.

There was great joy when they learned that Neil and Estelle would be marrying in February, and all vowed to make certain she had a memorable wedding day.

✌✙✙

Of course, Josephine had prayed that by some miracle, Andy would be granted leave for Christmas, but that wasn't to be.

140

Andy's Hurricane was strafed by a Luftwaffe aeroplane, and he was wounded in the leg. While it wasn't serious, he was confined to base hospital until after the New Year. Estelle had also hoped that Neil might be able to join her at Winthrop Manor for Christmas. Heavy fighting was taking place in both Italy and North Africa, and fresh troops were desperately needed. It was of vital importance that Neil finish his training so that he could be assigned to a permanent unit and begin to put his newly honed skills into practice. Thus, Estelle boarded a train and rode alone to Winthrop-on-Hart. The railroad cars were filled with soldiers on their way home for the holidays, and she tried not to cry because Neil wouldn't be by her side. She gazed out of the window and thought about all the changes that had taken place since she'd initially left home to attend The Sanford Institute.

18

Neil learned that his training would be finished on February 12, 1942. He was delighted to discover that he'd be given two weeks leave before receiving orders regarding where his unit would be assigned after training. He was beyond excited when he learned that the 1st Battalion, East Surrey Regiment was being reformed and would spend the next four months on home defence in expectation of a German invasion. That meant Neil would remain in England until the summer of 1942 after he and Estelle were married

His first task was to determine whether or not wives would be allowed at Chatham during that period. After speaking to the officer in charge of his regiment, he learned they could live off-base and he would report for duty each morning. Neil was delighted. He asked the commanding officer if he might be permitted to place a long-distance telephone call to Hampshire. He explained that he was planning marriage to his fiancée when his training was completed in February. The request was granted.

Estelle was at Winthrop Manor for Christmas when the telephone rang in the hallway. Being nearby, she ran to answer it. She had hoped with all her heart that Neil might at least be able to call her on the holiday.

She was overjoyed when she heard his voice. "Sweetheart," he said, "I have wonderful news!"

Estelle was overwhelmed just to hear his voice. "What Neil? Tell me your news."

"I won't be assigned to a posting after my training for a period approximately four months. I'll be staying here at Chatham Barracks to perform duties as a defender of the homeland in case the Germans decide to invade. That means you can move to Chatham, and we can live in a flat off base. I'll have to report for duty at the barracks each morning, but we'll be together. Isn't that wonderful news?"

Estelle was astounded. "Oh Neil, you can't be serious. You mean I won't have to say goodbye to you after we marry?"

"That's right, darling–at least not for four months. Perhaps if we're fortunate, the war will be over by then."

"Oh, what incredible news," she cried. "What about our marriage date? Have you learned when your training will be completed?"

"I finish my training on February twentieth. I'll be able to immediately catch a train to Hampshire. We can be married on your birthday, if that meets with your mother's approval. I've already written my parents, and they said it would be fine with them."

"Yes, yes!" Estelle shouted with glee. "I've already tried on Mum's wedding gown, and it needs just a few alterations. They are being taken care of now. I'll get together a list of guests to invite. You must do the same and send it to me. Have you a nice suit to wear?"

"Yes, of course, silly girl. I even have a black-tie ensemble, if you prefer that. Just because I grew up on a farm doesn't mean I'm lacking in knowledge about etiquette."

"Neil, I'm sorry. I knew that. My mum's gown is quite formal. It would be lovely if you were to wear something special. Mum and I will start to make all of the other necessary plans."

"Wonderful. Oh, and Estelle, my mother and father want me to send them your mother's address and telephone exchange. Mum wants to ring your mother."

"That would be lovely. Do you have that information?"

"Yes. I'll ring them tonight and let them have what they've requested. Shall I search for a flat for us to live in, or do you want to make that decision?" he asked.

"You can go ahead and find us a place. Then, take some pictures if you can, so I can figure out what we'll need in the way of furnishings."

"All right, my angel. I'm so happy. I *do* love you so."

"And I you, Neil. Thank you so much for the wonderful news. I can't wait to tell my mum. I'll write a long letter to you later tonight," Estelle promised.

Neil began to search at once for suitable accommodations for them to make their home. After a lengthy search, he was delighted to come upon a lovely Victorian house for lease on Maidstone Road in Chatham. He had been seeking a smaller flat, but when he discovered the house, he couldn't believe his luck. The owners had left their magical home at the beginning of the war to relocate to a cottage in the country. Chatham was not a tremendous distance from London, and the owners had been concerned about their safety after the Blitz. Because of its locale, the price was very reasonable. The house was absolutely delightful. Built in the 1890s, it had all the charm one would expect to find in a home of that era. Houses of that size and stature were a rare addition to the Chatham property market, positioned on one of the most sought-after roads in the area and located within a short walk of Chatham station. From the station, a person could travel to London's Victoria Station in under fifty minutes.

The house had three spacious bedrooms, a living and dining area, as well as an office, and even a library. There was a well-equipped kitchen and two bathrooms. The exterior was red brick with white columns. On top of those amenities, there was also a large, beautifully planted garden in the back. The lease price was more than Neil had planned to pay, but after a call to his parents, the decision was made that they would pay the rental price if Neil and Estelle would agree to let them move into the third bedroom. His parents wished to sell their farm in Wiltshire, since they were aging and weren't capable of the work required to keep it going. Another call was placed to Estelle, particularly to discuss whether she would be agreeable to his parents living with them. This was followed by several photographs of the house sent via post. After much discussion, an agreement was reached.

Estelle was keen on the prospect of having the Johnstons with them. She adored Neil's mother and felt she would provide companionship when Neil was on duty at Chatham Barracks, and afterwards, when he was undoubtedly posted abroad. The house was certainly large enough, and its design was such that one of the bedrooms and a water closet were on a different level than the other two, so the three people wouldn't feel as though they were on top of one another. The garden and sizable yard would keep Neil's father well-occupied and would also provide plenty of space for Estelle's beloved Petunia. Hence, the lease was signed and preparations were put into process for an anticipated move. The Johnstons sold their house rather quickly as many people were seeking property in the country because of the fear accompanying bombing in metropolitan areas. As a result, Neil's parents moved into the house on Maidstone Road before their son and Estelle were wed. The decision solved another problem for the young couple. There was more furniture than they could ever have afforded due to the sale of the farmhouse, so one more task was crossed off Neil and Estelle's list.

The Johnstons and Josephine were finally able to meet. Josephine planned a lovely weekend at Winthrop Manor complete with a dinner party, so everyone in the extended family would be given the opportunity to spend time together. Neil was granted leave for a weekend at the first of February. He had spoken to his parents about what sort of clothing would be suitable for the occasion.

The Johnstons had never imagined attending a dinner party at the home of a countess. They were still becoming accustomed to the fact that their son was marrying into such an aristocratic family. Neil's parents were by no means uneducated or down-market. In fact, both had grown up in London and had attended fine schools. They had fallen in love with the country and the idea of owning a farm had great appeal. Neil's mom, Lillian, had even participated in a London Season, which is where she had met her husband, Wayne Johnston. He had graduated from a fine men's college. However, shortly thereafter, his parents were killed in an automobile accident. Wayne inherited enough money to buy a farm in Wiltshire, and that was what Lillian and he chose to do. Lillian's family was infuriated at her choice and disowned her. She hadn't cared a whit. She and Wayne had spent many happy years on their farm, had one child, Neil, and were never sorry they'd left the possibility of a glamorous life. Still, that didn't mean they'd forgotten how to behave in a formal environment.

When the date for the dinner party arrived, Josephine couldn't help but remember the night when she'd met Win's parents for the first time. Josephine was adamant that such a horrendous scene would never be repeated at Winthrop Manor.

When the Johnstons arrived, accompanied by Neil, the family—including Elisabeth, Tom, Susan, Estelle, and Josephine—were dressed and ready to receive their guests. Estelle had been in a flutter all day, eagerly waiting to see Neil. She had dressed in a white wool dress, purchased long before the war. It was simple in design, with long sleeves and a square neckline. She wore only her engagement ring as jewelry. Josephine, who was nearly the same size she'd been when she married Win, wore a simple, elegant dress identical in colour to the pale, shell-pink gown she'd worn so long ago when first meeting Lord and Lady Winthrop. She so wished Andy could have been present, but she suspected he was somewhere over Italy at the time.

When the guests arrived, Estelle ran to Neil's arms, not caring at all if her behaviour was proper. No one else cared either. They kissed and held to each other as if they never wanted to be separated again. Neil looked extraordinarily handsome in a formal black-tie ensemble, as did his father, and Lillian was radiant in a lavender taffeta skirt with a white organdy top embroidered with tiny violets. Estelle was so proud of her soon-to-be in-laws. Josephine greeted them warmly, immediately erasing any uncomfortable feelings they may have harboured. The rest of the family followed suit.

They all made their way to the drawing room, where memories were like ghosts. Josephine knew that Win would have been so terribly proud of her abilities as a hostess. The evening was everything she had hoped it would be. Glancing at her daughter, she couldn't help being aware of the remarkable changes that had overtaken Estelle. She was the picture of happiness with Neil by her side, and it was obvious that Lillian and Wayne shared her feelings about the handsome couple.

When everyone proceeded to the dining room, the footmen held chairs for the ladies, and because of Andy's absence, Tom said grace. Elisabeth looked at him adoringly, thankful that he had been exempted from participation in the war due to the need for him to remain at his medical practice in Cloverdale. Without Tom, the many small villages in the area would have had no practicing physician for miles around. It had been his desire to join up and become a military doctor, but the powers that be judged his presence to be necessary in the small rural area.

Toasts were made to Estelle and Neil, Josephine as hostess, and tender reminiscences of Andy. The other brave Englishmen who were protecting their homeland were also remembered. Elisabeth's eyes momentarily filled with tears as she thought of her beloved first husband, Andrew, who had been killed in the Great War. Tom looked lovingly at his wife and understood her momentary sadness.

When the lavish dinner was over and it was time for the family and guests to retreat to their bed chambers, everyone felt as if they had become dear friends. There had been joy, sadness, and many memories shared, but most of all, happiness for Neil and Estelle reigned supreme.

The next day was unusually warm for early February. Neil and Estelle made their way to the stables where horses were saddled, and they set off on a long ride through the countryside. Estelle decided to show Neil the quaint cottage where her brother had lived with Josephine during the Great War. Neil immediately fell in love with it. Estelle had always dreamed of living in such a sweet bungalow, but the chances of that were very slim. Still, as the two rode back to the manor, the subject was discussed.

"You don't suppose your mother would allow us to set up housekeeping in the cottage, do you?" asked Neil.

"When, darling? You have to be in Chatham for four months," she replied.

"No. I mean after the war, Estelle. There's quite a lot of acreage there. We could raise our own sheep and crops."

"Gosh, I never even thought of such a thing," she answered. "Nevertheless, what about your parents? I hope we'll have children in time. There wouldn't be enough space."

"I suspect Mum and Dad will make an attempt to purchase the house in Chatham. If it can't be sold, I would bet my life they'll buy another house nearby. They already adore Chatham. I don't think they'll want to leave."

"Well," answered Estelle, "It's certainly something to think about. I'll ask Mummy what she thinks about the possibility."

When the couple returned to Winthrop Manor, Estelle sought out her mother. She found Josephine addressing wedding invitations in the library. Although Estelle had maintained that she would send simple, hand-written invitations, Josephine had extinguished that idea and ordered engraved vellum cards meant to be posted to every guest on the lists submitted by Lillian Johnston and Josephine herself. Naturally, Estelle and Neil had added friends of their own to the ever-growing number of invitees. What had begun as plans for an uncomplicated wedding had become an elegant affaire.

When Estelle entered the library, Josephine looked up and saw her daughter still clad in her riding clothes. Josephine placed her pen on the desk and smiled. "Hello, sweetheart. Did you and Neil enjoy your ride? Where did you go?"

"Oh, lots of places, Mummy, but the most fascinating was the darling cottage you and Elisabeth lived in during the war. The one that Win had built for you."

"Yes, it is quaint, isn't it?" Josephine responded. "If you'd told me you were going there, I'd have given you the key. It's still furnished. Did Neil like it?"

"Mummy, he loved it. He has the most wonderful idea, but I'm not certain you will be in favor of it," Estelle continued.

"Tell me what it is," Josephine asked.

"Neil thought that after the war, perhaps we could move to the cottage. We'd be able to have a farm and raise some sheep. Petunia could live with us there." Estelle smiled. "We're quite certain that Neil's parents will want to remain in Chatham. They seem to love it there. What are your feelings about the cottage?"

"Right now, that sounds like a first-rate plan. However, I don't think I'm in a position to answer definitely at the moment. Let's wait until this ghastly war has ended. There is also the possibility that Andy may have fallen in love and be married by then. Don't you see? This isn't the time to make such a decision."

"You're right, Mummy. I'll tell Neil that it would be better to wait until after the war to make this decision. I'll catch up with him before he leaves the stables. I left him to groom the horses since the stable boys are all off to the war. Poor old Jasper can't do everything alone."

19

❧❧

O n February 23, 1943, Estelle stood in the foyer of the chapel at Winthrop Manor. All of the guests had been seated and the ancient structure was filled to capacity. Estelle looked ravishing. All brides were supposed to be beautiful, but she had truly outdone herself. The dress she wore blended perfectly with the charming, sacred environment. It brought tears to Josephine's eyes to think that not only had she married Win in that enchanting dress, but her own mother wore the same charming gown when she'd vowed to love her father until death parted them.

Josephine wore a lavender taffeta gown, signifying that February was Estelle's birthday, and Lillian Johnston was garbed in a pale purple dress for the same reason. Neil's wedding gift to Estelle had been an amethyst necklace, bracelet, and earring suite to match her engagement ring. Estelle's bridesmaids wore white taffeta dresses, sprinkled with lavender violets.

The entire congregation had gasped with delight when they saw Estelle on Andy's arm, as the music for the procession began. Not even Estelle had known that he had been granted leave to escort his sister down the aisle. She'd had to brush away tears when he walked into the chapel. As the music began to play, Estelle clung to his arm, and Andy even had difficulty holding back tears of joy.

When they reached the altar, Father Comer asked who gave Estelle in marriage as Neil looked on, his heart bursting with love.

Andy answered, "Her mother and I do," just as Win would have, had he been present.

He passed Estelle to Neil and took a seat next to Josephine. Mother and son held hands throughout the ceremony. After Neil slipped the wedding ring consisting of a row of amethysts on Estelle's left hand, she replicated the act by placing a gold band on his left hand. They stepped up to the railing, knelt to pray, and communion was administered. At long last, Father Comer pronounced them man and wife. Neil lifted Estelle's veil and gently kissed her. As long as they lived, they never forgot that magical moment. The happiness dwelling in their hearts caused each to say a silent prayer for the thousands of soldiers around the globe with whom they would like to have shared their special moment. From that day forward, Estelle and Neil were certain that Private Neil Johnston and his wife were certain to have God's blessing, just as England was certain to be victorious.

ABOUT THE AUTHOR

Mary Christian Payne was highly successful in several management positions in Fortune 500 Companies, in New York City; St. Louis, Missouri; Orlando, Florida; and Tulsa, Oklahoma. Her work included Grant writing, and designing and writing training manuals for executive training programs.

She left the corporate world and became Director of Career Development at the Women' Resource Center at the University of Tulsa, where she designed a program that enabled hundreds of adult women to return to college and better their lives. She received the Mayor's Pinnacle Award in 1993 for this achievement. Mary left that position when the Center closed and then opened her own Career Counseling Center. She retired in 2008.

Mary Christian Payne became a successful, best-selling author at the age of 71 with the help of her publisher, Tom Corson-Knowles. All of her life, she had wanted to write and had received accolades for her unpublished work. She was encouraged in college, and writing was a significant part of the various jobs she held.

In 2013, she read Tom Corson-Knowles' book about publishing on Kindle. She wrote to him, and he telephoned her. The rest is history. Since that time, she has published nine books, with more on the way.

Mary lost her husband in June 2015, after 33 years of marriage. The grief process brought a lull to her writing, but she found that putting words on paper helped immensely. She is now in the process of writing her second novel since his death. She lives in Tulsa, Oklahoma with her two beloved Maltese dogs.

Sign up for the newsletter to get news, updates
and new release info from Mary Christian Payne:

www.TCKPublishing.com/mary

Other Books by Mary Christian Payne

The Somerville Trilogy
Willow Grove Abbey: Book 1 of the Somerville Trilogy
St. James Road: Book 2 of the Somerville Trilogy
Serendipity: Book 3 of the Somerville Trilogy

The Claybourne Trilogy
The White Feather: Book 1 of the Claybourne Trilogy
The White Butterfly: Book 2 of the Claybourne Trilogy
White Cliffs of Dover: Book 3 of the Claybourne Trilogy

The Thornton Trilogy
No Regrets: Book 1 of The Thornton Trilogy
No Gentleman: Book 2 of the Thornton Trilogy
No Secrets: Book 3 of the Thornton Trilogy

The Herrington Trilogy
Picture of Innocence: Book 1 of The Herrington Trilogy
Picture of Intrigue: Book 2 of the Herrington Trilogy
Picture of a Dream: Book 3 of the Herrington Trilogy

GET BOOK DISCOUNTS AND DEALS

Get discounts and special deals on our bestselling books at

www.TCKPublishing.com/bookdeals

www.ingramcontent.com/pod-product-compliance
Lightning Source LLC
Chambersburg PA
CBHW070959120726
47910CB00004B/1300